Scars Serve As Reminders

Will Appiah

Before the Crown

Scars Serve As Reminders

© 2022 William Appiah, New York City, NY

ISBN: 978-1-7326826-4-1

Crown Edition, 2022

Your scars are meant to remind you that you were stronger than whatever tried to hurt you.
-Unknown

I dedicate this novel to the person who taught me and the other teenyboppers how to find a voice. I wish you could see the person you helped me become. This is for you.

ab.

Also by Author:

The Purposeful Oliver Burke

The Angels Are Flying So Low

Table of Contents

"The wound is the place where the Light enters you."

-Rumi

Scars Serve As Reminders

PART I
I'M SORRY THAT IT'S TAKEN ME SO LONG...

CHAPTER 1:

HEAVY HEARTS

Oliver Burke   **Present Day**

"Hi Oliver. It's me. It's Lenny. Not sure if you remember me but... but... but I used to go by the dumb nickname, Lenox. Remember, Lenox Avenue in Harlem? I taught you that what seems like an eternity ago. Anyway, listen, man, I know it's been a long time..."

There was another pause in the message and as he listened, Oliver could hear the person on the other line clearing their throat while struggling to once again find their voice.

Oliver's palms began to moisten and for the first time in a long time, he could hear his heartbeat. He looked stiff and uncomfortable and peered over his shoulder anxiously but without focus as he grew suspicious. *What's going on?* When he was certain he was not being followed, he began to board the bus back home from the graveyard and listened as the voicemail continued.

"I know it's been a long while and the last time we seen each other was over thirty years ago. Man, I got a story for you and want to explain. There's a lot I need to tell you and I need to speak with you. Please give me a call back at this number. I really need to talk to you about this. Hope to hear from you soon man. Please."

Just then the voicemail abruptly cut off and Oliver's phone died. His heart was still beating much faster than he was comfortable with and using his moistened palms, he could feel the goosebumps that formed on his forearms. His body began to slowly tremble through a combination of his fear, doubt, and anger. He remembered exactly who Lenny was but sat in shock at the fact that a person he hadn't seen or heard from since his teen years in Brooklyn suddenly decided to reappear and reach out. Worst of all, he knew Lenny as the only known relative of Rahzmel Davis. The man who murdered Oliver's mother, Mabel-Ara Burke. The thought of this alone angered him.

Lenny? Why the hell is he calling me? Why now?

He sat bewildered and concerned. Although they were once best friends, Oliver associated Lenny's sudden disappearance with the reason he ended up at the gang's clubhouse that day. He believed Lenny was responsible for him giving away his freedom in exchange for a place within Rahzmel's ranks.

No…no…I don't want to go back to that time, he thought to himself. *My life's already perfect and the last thing I need is to be reminded of a past plagued with emptiness and deceit.*

Oliver's thoughts were scattered and when he finally found a seat on the crowded bus, he attempted to settle his racing mind by focusing on anything but Lenny's voicemail.

The moon was nice tonight, he thought. *What a beautiful night.*

Living in Manhattan, Oliver hadn't seen the moon that way in a long time. From his aisle seat, he stared out of the window and watched as it silently stared at the seemingly empty New York cemetery that October night. It created a light coat of fog that had formed between gravestones and stretched in perfect alignment for acres in every direction. The moisture in the air made it a cool place to be that morning and after one of the warmest nights that year, this was exactly the reprieve New York needed. The earthy smell of fresh-cut grass paired well with the moistened soil which made the seemingly empty graveyard feel like home.

I'll miss this, he thought as the bus pulled away for its hour and a half ride back to Port Authority Bus Terminal.

*****

Hearing this voicemail from Lenny took Oliver's mind back to a place he hadn't recalled in a while. The day of his adoption was intended to be the happiest day of his teenage years but instead was one of the darkest nights. The day his entire family was taken from him and the only true happiness, acceptance, and belonging he'd experienced up until that point became extinct. In his dream, he was taken back to the day of the house fire. The day Lenny's cousin, Rahzmel Davis, took everything from him.

His mind drifted back to the entire scene from the fire which took the lives of his adoptive brothers, sisters, and his mother, Mabel-Ara. In his dream, he could smell the putrid stench of burning wood, plastic, and dust. The flames tore down the only place he called home, section by section until it was no more than rubble and ashes. He vividly remembered the blistering heat and how it had left a permanent pink and purple scar on his arm that day. The fire also left him with something the world couldn't see. Something that trapped his mind and heart for years until therapy and time played their parts towards his recovery.

He felt himself growing anxious and let out a low and intermittent whimper. All the emotion he'd experienced that day suddenly rushed through his being and he felt a heaviness in his heart. Although this was just a dream, it affected him deeply. He hadn't dreamed like that in years and at that moment, he believed Lenny's return couldn't be good.

As the dream continued and Oliver was about to be rescued from the fire, he felt his body suddenly shaking. When he opened his eyes, he realized the bus had finally arrived at Port Authority and he was being woken up. When he looked over, he could see the impatience in the face of the lady sitting beside him and rubbed his eyes to ensure he was awake. When he realized where he was and that his dream was over, he quickly gathered his belongings and then began to stand up to get in line to depart.

"I'm sorry. I was just…"

"Hurry up, man," the lady interrupted. "I cannot miss the train back to New Jersey."

She forced herself through the little space available between her and each passenger lined up to depart until she was completely off the bus. Oliver watched this from his seat and could see the shock on the faces of the other passengers by her blatant act of disregard. Although he understood their concern, Oliver empathized with the lady and understood her haste. His commute was almost two hours each way which meant he was in transit for close to four hours in total each shift. One miss of a train or bus would extend that, and he was tired of it. He knew subconsciously that he was beginning to answer the questions he'd asked himself earlier that night and felt his decision was already made—but still planned to speak with Amerie about everything.

CHAPTER 2:

WALK IN YOUR SHADOW

Oliver Burke

As he arrived back at the empty house, Oliver saw Amerie had already left for work but prepared him breakfast and a note. When he read the note, he was quickly reminded that any time spent with Amerie was more important than any amount of money he would ever earn.

Heading to work but made you breakfast. Got your message this morning but your phone must have died. Can't wait to see you later babe. Love you! ☺

Oliver melted at her thoughtfulness and knew how lucky he was. He hadn't had the best luck with women over the course of his life and saw Amerie as complete. She was beautiful, intelligent, and caring, and Oliver was certain that he was the luckiest guy in the world. Her brunette hair always had a glow to it that complimented her dark eyes, fair skin, and curvy figure. She took care of herself, and Oliver wanted to ensure he could offer her what she deserved in a man—a partner.

He continued with his day and focused on completing the house chores before Amerie came home to make up for his unusual night out. He'd never stayed out all night like that and wanted to apologize by taking care of everything, so she didn't have to lift a finger when she returned.

By the time Amerie finally came home that evening, Oliver rushed over in excitement, catching her before she could even close the door. His conversation with Walter at the cemetery was fresh on top of his mind and seeing his pain reminded Oliver to act on what mattered.

It's so important that I tell and show her how I feel because we never know in this life. Which days may be our last.

He couldn't imagine his life without her. Before she could even put her purse down, he went in for a long passionate kiss and stared deeply into her eyes.

"I love you," he remarked excitedly.

"Ooohhh... hi baby," she exchanged in surprise with a big smile. "I love you too. What's that for?"

"I missed you and I'm very sorry about last night. It kind of got away from me and by the time I checked my phone, it was morning. Then it died. How was work?"

He grabbed her jacket and bag and walked her over to the bedroom to get cleaned up.

"It was good. I was nervous last night when you didn't come home. I saw your text message this morning, but you can't do that again, babe. You had me so worried. What exactly happened?"

"I know and I'm sorry about that. I promise it won't happen again. I was working my normal shift when something miraculous happened."

She stared in anticipation. "What happened?!? Don't leave me in suspense."

"So, before my shift, I had been telling myself I didn't want to be a gravedigger anymore. The work sucks, the commute is long, and worst of all, I'm away from you *all* day. I'm really tired every day and yesterday before my shift, I really wanted to take a sick day.

"Something in me said, '*not today.*' It wasn't like a voice or anything like that. Just that I no longer felt good calling off, so I sucked it up and forced myself to go to work. I knew nothing would be any different today, than yesterday or the day before but still dragged myself back to that damn graveyard."

He paused to take a breather as she wiped her hands and followed her into the next room.

"Strangely... the shift was different. Very different actually. While working, I heard a voice, faintly and in the distance speaking out. The voice was speaking openly into the air but at that moment, I swear to you, I felt the wind suck out the space between me and the other person. It was like they were speaking directly to me and nothing or no one else was there.

"I felt compelled to explore the source of the voice, so I walked toward its direction and when I finally found it, I felt an unusual feeling of joy and shock. It was like that feeling of finding the missing piece of a puzzle that you thought you lost but knew you needed to complete the greater picture. A pure feeling of elation. Anyway... It's hard to explain but..."

She interrupted nervously. "Tell me! Who was it?"

"Okay... okay! Sorry," he giggled. "It was Walter Benine. It was the man that I told myself I needed to find and after searching through what felt like was every corner of Manhattan. The man whose shadow I walked in for months. The man who was everywhere I needed to be but was nowhere that I was. I found him in the last place I could've imagined. A graveyard in Upstate New York that I almost wasn't going to be at yesterday. I was shocked, and a little scared, but knew I was exactly where I needed to be at that moment."

"Oh my God. How was he? He looked bad when we saw him on tv."

"He was hurt, babe. Really hurt. He seemed in a truly dark place and at first, I struggled with how I could help him. I could barely remember everything I'd told myself I wanted to tell him, and it wasn't until the moment I stared into his eyes and could see my eighteen-year-old self staring back at me that the words finally flowed. The conversation was such an emotional roller-coaster, I can recall everything we both said—word for word.

"I told him pieces of my story and the people who impacted me. He told me about the death of his girlfriend and about his brother, who he also thought was dying, but I think he may have been wrong. We spoke through the night, into this morning, and at the end of our conversation..." He froze as he remembered back.

"Oh shoot... at the end of our conversation, I told him I would be there to visit him and his brother at the hospital, but I forgot. How could I forget?" Oliver slapped his forehead with both palms and wiped them down his face.

"Be there to visit?"

"Yes! Remember, I went looking for Walter and found his brother, Justice, instead? Well, when I was with Walter last night, I promised I would go see them both in the hospital, but I forgot! How could I forget?"

"People forget things all the time, babe. I'm sure Walter will understand. Let's plan to go see them at some point tomorrow."

They were now sitting on the same side of the bed, and she listened intently. He loved her for the support she'd always shown him, even when he didn't believe he deserved it. As they sat, she placed her arm around his lowered shoulders and rested her head on his. Oliver was now looking down at his hands, his left wringing his right.

"Actually…I think I know why. It was probably because of what happened next. When I looked at my phone, I saw your calls and voicemail, and saw a call and voicemail from Lenny."

His voice almost dropped to a whisper in his revelation as he turned his body and looked at her.

"Lenny? Your friend you told me about from your childhood? The one who disappeared, and you went looking for then found his cousin?"

"Yes, that's him."

Oliver paused as he felt his head growing warm.

"Babe. I don't like this. I don't like it one bit." Her hands were now covering her mouth and she slowly shook her head. "What made him your best friend, anyway? Sounds like you were only together a short while."

"We spent a lot of time together. It didn't span years like some friendships do but what we had felt deeper. He was exactly like me, and I think that's what bonded us. I think his absence made me realize how much of an impact he made on me in that short time. When I tried to make friends, I struggled because no one else was like us. All the other kids were so different, and I always felt judged, used, or that people feared me. I guess that's what came with living in the foster house."

"That makes more sense," she offered. "I've had friends like that too, but this guy sounds like bad news."

"I'm still torn though. I don't know what Lenny wants but what I do know is that he's the reason I joined the gang in the first place." Oliver paused again as he caught himself raising his voice in anger. Amerie could see he was remembering the feeling of abandonment he felt after Lenny's disappearance and placed his hands in hers. They were not as cold as they normally were but were clammy and full of callus.

"He didn't really give me any details. From what I could tell, it wasn't because he couldn't remember, it felt like he didn't want to. At least not over the phone. He asked to meet."

Amerie sat speechless, slowly shaking her head. Oliver could sense she was connecting to his story and before he could continue, she interjected.

"Well, you said no, right?"

"I didn't return the call. He sounded different from how I remembered him and if it's really the same Lenny from our childhood, I think I need to call him back. There are so many questions I have for him starting with where he's been."

She snatched her hands back and rose to her feet in shock. She wore confusion on her face, and it was obvious she wasn't supportive of his plans.

"What are you saying? Tell me you're not planning to call him, right?"

Oliver sat silent. His lack of response quickly made Amerie grow uneasy. "Right?!?"

"I'm not sure, babe!" the volume in his voice rose in frustration as he also rose to his feet and walked to the opposite side of the room. "It's been over thirty years and I don't know. I feel I need answers."

Amerie shook her head in disappointment. "Need answers? … It's been thirty years and I'm sure a lot has changed but the last time you saw each other was when you were kids. Neither of you is the same person you were back then so what answers could you possibly need that will affect your life for the better?"

"I know but I need to know what happened."

"And then what? You'll feel fulfilled? Feel like you've gotten closure? I don't care if it's been thirty days or thirty years, please don't return that phone call."

He had a demure look on his face and stared straight into her eyes. He saw she was on the verge of tears and went to wipe them with his sleeve, but she pulled away.

"I don't know but you don't need to worry about me. Even if I do speak to him again, I won't ever go back to that dark place again. Not ever."

"And what if it's not your choice?" she questioned in annoyance as her voice raised. Her cheeks were now flushed, and it was obvious she was frustrated with how much resistance he was giving her on this matter. "What if he tells you something that upsets you? Who will save you then, huh? It's going to end up being me and Dr. Novak."

"I don't think it will come to that. I only want answers."

"But things are going well right now. Our life's not perfect but we worked hard to get here. Why do you want to disrupt that in search of answers that frankly, you don't even know the questions to!" she roared back.

Oliver watched as she caught herself. "I don't think you'll find the answers you're looking for," she said, more calmy. "We're partners here and I'm here to help you but only can if you let me. Please don't do this."

"I know!" He shot back. "I know we're partners."

"Do you? Cause it sounds like you're about to make a dumb decision because of your desire to be there for everyone. It's good that you want to help but some people really need to save themselves."

Oliver remained silent. His word meant everything to him, and he didn't want to lie to her about his feelings or plans with Lenny. He didn't want to mislead her in order to avoid a difficult conversation and simply remained quiet, so she continued.

"Well know this…you want to get answers, I don't care anymore. You say we're partners but don't even consider how this affects me. I can't even look at you right now. I need some sleep and the couch has your name on it."

She handed him a pillow and got into bed, quickly switching off the light on the bedside. Oliver didn't want her to sleep upset but could sense their conversation wasn't going any further tonight.

Guess I'll leave it alone tonight. Maybe we both just need time to cool down.

He went in to kiss her, just as he'd done every night since they began dating, but she quickly turned her body around to face the opposite side of the room and pulled the covers up.

Instead, he kissed the side of her head and whispered in her ear, "I'm sorry and I love you," then motioned towards the door. From the door frame, he could hear her sniffling in the darkness and made one final remark. "I don't want you to go to bed upset. Please talk to me."

She remained silent and just before he walked out, she turned around so he could only see the silhouette of her craned head staring at him in the dark.

"I'm not upset, just disappointed."

Just before he closed the bedroom door, he gave one final look back and dropped his head on his way to the living room couch.

I hate to upset her like this, but I won't be able to move on until I get this closure. Maybe one of us will feel different in the morning. I hope so.

With that, Oliver found himself alone on the living room couch and stared at the moon through the floor-to-ceiling windows for hours until it finally carried him into sleep.

CHAPTER 3:

SANCTUARY

Oliver Burke

Oliver was awoken just before 6 a.m. by the sun's rays which pierced through the living room's translucent window blinds. Their New York City apartment was on a high floor of their luxury building and had incredible views facing the East River. On most mornings, the rays from the rising sun bounced off of the water perfectly and produced an illuminating hue that brightened their entire apartment. This sheen usually set each day off on the right foot.

Unfortunately, this was not one of those mornings. Although the sun's rays were present, Oliver was still thinking about how upset Amerie was the night before and already felt as if the day had set off on the wrong foot. He regretted causing her so much anger but knew he needed answers that neither she nor Dr. Novak could provide.

When he peered over at the clock on the wall, he realized he'd only slept for two hours and was exhausted. He wasn't used to sleeping on the couch for long periods and struggled as he forced himself up.

Ughhh…

He was weary and wanted to go back to sleep but knew he couldn't go back to bed with things the way they were. He needed to address his fight with Amerie and made a follow-up conversation a priority for this morning.

I've never seen her that upset. I hope she'll talk to me this morning.

Oliver thought back to the advice he'd received from his mother. *Don't ever go to bed upset or be the reason someone else does.*

He shook his head in embarrassment at the fact that he hadn't followed his mother's advice and had been the cause of this for Amerie. He went to the bedroom hoping to apologize and get some extra sleep, but when he opened the door, he noticed the bed was made and she was gone. She'd left for work early, which was his indication that she was still upset with him. He checked his phone and noticed he had a text from her sent at 3:45 a.m. which was much earlier than her normal scheduled shift.

Left for work early. Have a good day.

So, he responded.

Thanks, Babe – Heading to the center today but first I'm going to stop by the hospital. See you soon.

*****

Before going to the youth center in Brooklyn, Oliver made one stop at New York-Presbyterian hospital in lower Manhattan where Amerie worked. He had visited numerous times before and knew exactly where to find her. He was still unsure about his plans with Lenny but knew he needed to mend things with Amerie. That took precedence.

This hospital was also where he'd previously come looking for Walter Benine, but found his brother, Justice, instead. During his visit, Justice had encountered a head injury while saving others from an attack and seemed like he was on the road to recovery. For that reason, Oliver was shocked when Walter revealed his brother was close to death. Based on their graveyard conversation, he knew something terrible had occurred.

When he arrived on the floor Amerie worked on, Oliver watched as she bounced from room to room, seeing patients and their families during each visit. The floor was busy and it was now obvious to him that this wasn't an ideal time to speak so he continued to stare at her from a distance.

She's so beautiful, he thought. *Doing what she enjoys. Helping people. That's what matters.*

After a few minutes of staring impassively, she finally saw him standing beside the pillar located near the bank of elevators. When they connected eyes, he watched a big smile form on her face, which he used as an invitation to approach, and he reciprocated the expression with a smile of his own.

"I'm so sorry, babe. I don't like how upset I made you last night and especially didn't want you to go to bed mad."

"I wasn't mad at you," she admitted placing her hands inside of his. "I worry for you and don't think you're making the right decision to connect with Lenny. I know you want to save the world but perhaps it's important to protect your peace instead and let some things be."

He looked befuddled. "Trust me. My peace is the one thing I don't want to lose. Especially after we worked so hard to find it."

Oliver could tell she wanted to share more but just as she was attempting to do so, one of her colleagues came and pulled her away. "Amerie, Mr. Scofield is asking for you."

"Okay, thanks. I'll be right there."

Without saying a word, she turned back to Oliver and simply stared. She had a pensive look on her face that she'd displayed numerous times before and smiled at the gesture of Oliver's visit. He could tell she wanted to talk more but needed to get back to work and reassured her. "I'll give it more thought before doing anything, deal?"

"Okay." Before she could finish, Amerie quickly turned away and rushed away to Mr. Scofield's room when she heard ringing coming from his monitor.

I love her more than anything and maybe she's right. Maybe I'm being stupid even wanting to speak to Lenny again, but I can't run from it. I need to address this head-on.

Once Amerie was gone, Oliver made his way up to the same room he'd found Justice in days before. The floor seemed busy, but not like the floor Amerie worked on. The room assigned to Justice was located in the middle of a long hallway and was around the corner from the bank of elevators, which allowed Oliver to visit the room without passing too many people.

When he arrived on the floor and exited the elevator, Oliver saw Walter at the end of the hall sauntering in his direction. At the same moment that Walter saw him, he beamed in excitement and picked up his pace. He had a look of familiar excitement that came from reconnecting with an old friend.

Seeing Walter this way brought Oliver a surge of happiness. He looked much better than he did at the graveyard and Oliver could tell something was different. He wasn't sure what it was at the moment but was happy to see it.

Wow – He's beaming.

Walter could barely contain his joy and went in for a big bear hug when he'd arrived at Oliver's location. "You came!"

"Yes! I said I would, and wanted to be here with you and Justice. I try not to don't break promises. How did everything go? Is he okay?"

"Yeah! He's all good now," Walter stated with happiness glowing. "Let's go in."

Upon their entry, Justice turned his attention from the TV towards the door and looked in surprise. He still had a bandage on his head but seemed sprightlier than he was when Oliver last saw him. He jumped out of bed as the two men approached and traded glances between them.

He could barely conceal his delight. "I'm glad you finally found each other. I wasn't sure how I was going to keep pretending I didn't know him." He then turned to Oliver. "Good to see you again, bro," he offered with an accompanying handshake, which he pulled in for a hug.

"Good to see you too, young man. Heard the last few days have been pretty rough. You doing okay?"

"I'm great! Thanks for coming. Everything okay with you?"

"Yeah, everything's okay," he lied.

Oliver's mind was still conflicted on how he wanted to handle the Lenny situation. He felt like he was in a slightly better place with Amerie but knew there was still work to do there. He didn't know Walter or Justice well but from what he did know about them, they were smart, talented young men and he believed he could confide in them.

Maybe they can help me make a decision, he thought. He felt comfortable in their presence and continued.

"Actually…I could be better, to be honest," he admitted looking around the room. His eyes fixated on two chairs near the bed. "Can we sit?"

"Of course." Justice switched off the television and also turned his attention to Oliver, matching his brother who was already seated in one of the chairs.

Oliver looked around without focus for a moment. It felt like he was *just* at the cemetery with Walter playing the role of the "strong friend" and giving him advice on how to handle his own insecurities. Now, he was the one who needed help. He wasn't a proud man but still wanted to be a strong friend to the two brothers, so he began slowly, in a premeditated way, to ensure he wasn't unloading on them.

"Well after we spent the night talking in the cemetery, I got a call from an old friend who I knew when we were kids. He left me a voicemail and sounded as if he was in rough shape. At least from what I could tell over the phone."

"So, what's bothering you," Justice interjected in confusion. "Doesn't sound like much of a problem to me."

"Well, that's it. This friend had a lot going on back then and ended up disappearing. Now he's back apparently and looking to reconnect. The problem is that in the time since he's been gone, I had to deal with a lot. Too much to mention right now but a lot has happened, and my girlfriend, Amerie, is worried about me speaking with him."

Justice still looked confused, but Oliver could tell Walter understood where he was coming from. They'd spent the entire night speaking about pain, healing, and love, and Walter wore sympathy in his look.

"What does he want from you?" the young socialite questioned.

"I'm not sure and that's what bothers me. I kind of want answers from him. I have so much on my mind and don't think I'll stop thinking about this until I get those answers."

"Have you explained to her?" Justice chimed.

"Yes, I have. She's against me even reaching back out to him because she thinks it's going to undo everything I fixed in therapy. She says the risk is far too high and outweighs any possible reward. She doesn't believe meeting him will affect my life for the better."

Walter held understanding in his stare. "Well, maybe he's not supposed to affect your life for the better here. Maybe he reached out because he *needs* you to affect him for the better. Similar to how you did my life."

Oliver was so impressed with his resolve and insight. "Yes – I'm feeling like that also."

Justice interjected when he finally understood. "Nah, I think your girlfriend is right. Why would you go back to that? Sounds like nothing but problems to me."

Walter shook his head then suddenly pulled out his phone and clicked on a link saved onto his favorites. Just as he handed the phone to Oliver, he read the title of the article out loud.

"Brooklyn Man Returns Home to Open Youth and Development Center," he beamed with joy as he continued. "You said you did all the research on me before finding me in the cemetery. Well since we left, I did a little research on you and came to find this article published about you opening up a youth and development center? Wow! When we talk about affecting people's lives for the better, you're already doing it. Why should you treat this situation with your friend any different than you treat those kids? Seems to me they both need you."

He has a point, Oliver admitted to himself. *He doesn't know about Lenny's relationship with Rahzmel though. Maybe I need to give him that perspective.*

"Well, there's a little more to it. This friend I'm talking about is related to the man who killed my mother. He's his cousin."

Both Walter and Justice looked stunned by the revelation. Their mouths were open and eyebrows raised. "Oh!"

It was no surprise that Oliver could see the shock painted all over Justice's face but in Walters's look, he didn't see shock. He saw comprehension. Their night in the graveyard had revealed many truths and to Walter, this was one of the many that made Oliver the strong and courageous individual he was. He continued.

"And your friend was involved? Was he also responsible for your mother's death? Is that why he disappeared?"

"I'm not sure. I don't think he was because he went missing long before it happened," Oliver acknowledged. "It was actually years before if I recall. I'm not even sure if he knows."

He watched as Walter traded glances with Justice. No words were said, and Oliver knew both of them were deliberating, in their minds, the right words to say to bring him comfort. After a brief moment, Walter turned back to Oliver. "I'm not going to pretend to have all the answers or know what you're dealing with but you helped me the other night so I will share my point of view. Hopefully, it helps." He cleared his throat. "I think your friend may just want to reconnect or explain what happened. Perhaps he needs this as atonement for leaving. Maybe it will be helpful, maybe not. You won't know unless you call him back."

"And if it's not helpful?"

"Then you keep killing it at life. You're already doing so much and helping a lot of people. If this one conversation isn't helpful or hurts you, it sounds like there are tons of people in your life to help you. Including the two of us."

"Yeah. All that makes sense. Life's all about chances and if it doesn't go your way, we got you, bro!" Justice pronounced enthusiastically.

Oliver's mood lightened as he stood impressed at their maturity and wisdom.

"Thanks, guys. I should be heading out. I'm heading to the youth center now and have some work to do but I really appreciate y'all. More than you know. I'm proud of you."

He was paralyzed with happiness and didn't want to end their conversation but knew he needed to go. "You guys should come by some time. Would be great for the kids to meet you. I think they'll be inspired by all you both do. Just like I am."

"That would be great. Thanks, Oliver. We'll plan on it."

The three men then exchanged phone numbers and Oliver departed.

*****

As Oliver made his way through the brightly lit hallways of the Youth and Development Center, he was overjoyed by the sight of happiness on the faces of the kids he passed. Many who moseyed through the hallway were preteens, much younger than he was when he met Lenny, and he could sense they hadn't seen half of what he saw by the time he was their age. As an orphan, he had bounced from house to house by the time he was getting to his teen years and carried a shield of anger intended to protect himself. Back then, he didn't know that this same shield would be the armor that attracted others with nefarious intentions toward him.

Now, more than thirty years later, he found excitement in the things that remained the same about kids in Brooklyn and was intrigued by the things that were vastly different. Like him, most who came to the center grew up in Brooklyn and walked with a swagger one could only inherit through generations of citizenship in the borough.

These kids still walk around like their parents and grandparents used to.

He laughed to himself and stopped in the doorway of one of the training rooms, as an activity was going on. From his spot, he watched as the volunteers engaged a younger class of children in a rousing game of Duck Duck Goose.

Without saying a word, he quietly made his way into the circle of children and sat beside two he hadn't seen before. One was a Hispanic boy with a short buzzcut and earrings in both ears. He had a faint outline of a mustache and Oliver could tell he was months, if not weeks, away from becoming a man. The other preteen was a fair-skinned girl with curly brunette hair, which resembled Amerie's. He could tell at least one of her parents was white and the other had a darker complexion. He smiled as he sat between them. Like the others sitting around the cluster, he turned his attention to the participant actively circling the group tapping "duck" on each head he passed. When someone finally selected the goose, the room erupted in cheers as both children ran around until the designated selector stole the seat from their victim.

I hope I don't get selected, he thought. *I don't move like I used to.*

Before he could even finish his thought, his head was tapped. He stumbled getting to his feet and by the time he'd begun to accelerate, the person who'd selected him was already more than 3/4 around the circle.

"Who do you think you are, old man?" a voice jested from the doorway. When Oliver looked over, he saw a friend, Officer Jalacie Jefferson, with a big smile on his face.

"I thought I could be young again but guess my body doesn't agree." He then turned back and connected his eyes with the Hispanic boy. "You take my turn. Reclaim my honor."

The teen giggled as Oliver and Jalacie walked away.

"This place looks better every day."

"Yeah, the kids are flocking here from all over Brooklyn. It's really something special. Imagine if something like this was around when you were coming up."

"I know. Imagine that."

"How's Amerie?"

"We had a little fight."

"About what? Your cooking? the officer traded with a playful shove.

"Nah – it was nothing serious. Just us being a couple."

"Well don't upset her. Don't forget I'm the one who introduced you."

"Yeah, yeah. I remember."

"Good," Jalacie remarked as they walked up to a portrait that hung on the main office wall.

IN HONOR OF MABEL-ARA BURKE.

Both Oliver and Jalacie stared at the portrait until Jalacie turned to Oliver.

"Would you have done it any different if we could? Running this place and volunteering?"

Oliver smiled back.

"Nah, we're doing it exactly how Ma did it. The way it's supposed to be. We're keeping her sanctuary alive. That's what matters."

CHAPTER 4:

IT'S ALWAYS BEEN YOU

Oliver Burke

Over the course of the days which followed, Oliver thought more about what he wanted to do and as each day passed, he felt closer to making a decision. The reassurance he received from Justice and Walter proved helpful and he now needed to find a way to convince Amerie, who hadn't spoken with him much since their argument. He knew she worried for him but didn't want that to prevent him from at least calling Lenny back.

There is a risk in calling but I feel there's a greater risk in not.

Taking risks had become something very important to him. He believed every moment from Mabel-Ara opening her home to him fresh out of prison to his two guardian angel officers who risked their lives and jobs to ensure he was taken care of time and time again. Everything started with risk, and he began to realize he needed to take one also even if it meant he may be making the wrong decision.

*****

By the end of his fourth day of deliberating, Oliver felt ready to move forward with a decision. He'd been avoiding Lenny since the original voicemail and saw that he had numerous missed phone calls, voicemails, and unanswered text messages. It was obvious to Oliver that Lenny was desperate to connect.

He'd already quit working at the graveyard and was now planning to work full time in the youth center. The money was no longer important to him, and he was tired of trading it for things he didn't feel passionate about.

There's more I'm supposed to do here than chase money.

That night, when Amerie arrived home, he sat her down in the kitchen for another conversation while he prepared dinner for the two of them.

"Before you say anything, please listen," he began. "My life hasn't been easy and there are lots of things in my past that I wish I could change, including joining a gang, but the fact of the matter is I can't. I was broken and lost until two officers made a call to Mabel-Ara and gave me a fighting shot in life. Mabel-Ara picked up their call and my life sort of began on that day."

He poured her a glass of her favorite white wine to compliment the crudité platter he'd placed in front of her. She was picking at the raw vegetables and had her eyes concentrated. Oliver could tell she was itching to say something from her look and continued before she had a chance.

"Even though I was not the ideal candidate for adoption, Mabel-Ara picked up the call. There were obvious red flags in my past that should have caused her to turn around and run but she picked up. I didn't tell you this but on my first night at Mabel-Ara's home, she caught me stealing things from her, and just as I was about to sneak out of the house, she stopped me. She didn't accuse me or shame me for stealing her belongings."

His heart felt heavy speaking about Mabel-Ara, and he held gratitude in his look. "No, instead she took a different approach. She asked if I *'have everything I need'* and gave me a chance to decide what type of person I wanted to be. I know she saw me take her things, but she taught me a valuable lesson that day. She showed me that I can be someone people can trust if I allow myself to be. She simply picked up..."

Oliver walked over and stood by her side. He could smell her Chanel perfume and see her eyes were concentrated on his lips, so he placed both hands on hers and whispered.

"Mabel-Ara picked up for me when she didn't need to. I think I need to pick up for Lenny."

Oliver then retracted his hands and wiped the corners of his eyes which were swelled with tears he was fighting to hold back. He touched the permanent scar on his tricep, which was his reminder of the sacrifice Mabel-Ara made for him on the day she died in the house fire. When Amerie saw this, she slowly moved his hand and kissed the burn. He melted in her warmth and continued.

"I'm sure I'm going to be different after my conversation with him, but I welcome it. It's this type of uncertainty that makes life exciting. I'm not angry with him like I was back then and if this ends up going wrong, it will be a lesson learned."

Amerie remained silent, and Oliver could see she was still itching to get a word in so he stopped and stared.

"You've been the most remarkable man I've met in my life. You care so much for others, and it inspires me. You tend to wear the weight of the world on your shoulders, and I've seen, firsthand, how it strains you."

Oliver stood silent waiting for her to continue her objection but was surprised by what she said next.

"But if you think a conversation with Lenny needs to happen, I won't be a barrier for you. My number one priority is you and I only ask that you go in with your eyes open, so you don't let him mislead you. Remember, he's still Rahzmel's cousin."

"Yes, I know. I won't let that happen. I've held so much anger towards him for most of my life, yet I don't truly know why. I'm going to call him tomorrow and take it from there. Hopefully, I'll get my questions answered. After that, I plan to close this chapter and move on."

"Okay, babe," she remarked as he finished preparing them dinner. "If he really needs something, don't forget, there are also others who can help him. It doesn't always need to be you."

*****

The following morning, Oliver woke up in their shared bedroom and noticed Amerie had already left for work again. Thankfully, she was scheduled on her normal morning shift that day and he woke up content knowing she did not leave the house upset. Even though she didn't fully support his plans, she supported him and for that he was grateful.

Why do I feel so nervous? He thought. *I need to let him do the talking. Even though I'm not angry, he has a lot to explain.*

Oliver disregarded all the missed text messages and voicemails and finally dialed Lenny back. Almost immediately after the first dial tone had ended, there was a response.

"Hello…Oliver? Thanks for calling me back," Lenny started in a sickly manner which indicated he was not fully awake or not 100% healthy.

"Is this really you?" Oliver questioned shortly.

"Yes, it's me. It's Lenny from Brooklyn. Well… originally Lenny from Harlem. I appreciate you calling me back. I just—"

"What do you want?" Oliver interrupted loudly. He paced the living room anxiously. The malaise that had passively gripped him for over thirty years had returned. "You disappeared and now you're what? Calling to check in?" He felt himself raising his voice and paused. He took a long breath and stopped to look at the sun's reflection as it bounced off the East River, then said. "To be honest, I'm not even sure who I'm talking to."

"Listen, Oliver, I know you have a lot of questions and I hope I have answers to all of them but yes, it's really me. It's the same Lenny who showed you the secret door to leave through the gym at Roman Reade high school. Remember?" He continued.

"It's the same Lenny who taught you all about Harlem and used to bust your ass in ball." He coughed to clear his throat before he proceeded.

"It's the same Lenny that found you wandering the hallways, like me, and instantly knew we were meant to be friends. Best friends actually. Yeah, Oliver—it's me."

"Lenny, what happened to you? Where have you been all this time?"

"I'm glad you called me back, man. There's so much to say. Can we meet? There's a lot we need to talk about, and I think it will be better if we meet."

"I don't know if that's a good idea. After thirty years, you show back up and now you want to meet? Just tell me what you need to say."

"I get it. I just disappeared and trust me, there's a very long story there but I'd prefer to speak in person. Please, man. Can we do that?"

"I don't know. I don't know if that's a good idea."

"Please, Oliver. Please. I spent a long time searching for you and there's a lot I need to say. A lot I need to share about what happened to me. It wouldn't cut it over the phone. Please?"

Oliver felt the conversation going nowhere and interrupted, "listen, man. I need to go but give me some time to think through this. I'll let you know soon if we can meet."

"Okay, Oliver. Please let me know."

Just before Oliver hung up, Lenny cleared his throat one last time and made one final comment.

"Wait…I'm sorry for what he did to you…"

At that moment, the phone dial clicked, and Oliver sat unsatisfied.

What he did to me? What does he mean? Rahzmel? That was his cousin. What does he know about what he did to me?

Oliver left their brief conversation with more questions than answers and felt conflicted. Hearing Lenny's voice made him realize how much more he needed to learn about what happened and he struggled with how he would get it. He'd already taken a risk in calling him back and wanted that to be enough but knew there was more to it. He could sense there was more Lenny wanted to say but he didn't over the phone. If he wanted to learn more, which he did, he needed to go see Lenny.

*****

When Amerie arrived back home that evening, she found Oliver in the kitchen sitting on the computer, with his back facing her. He did not hear her come in and she could smell the short ribs he had braising on the stove. She quietly motioned behind him and covered his eyes.

"Guess who?"

"The biggest pain in my butt?"

"You wish!" she said as she kissed the crown of his head and went to lower the stove. "Smells good. Uh oh...why are you being so nice and cooking such a special dinner?"

"Was it that obvious?! I figured since I'm not working right now, I can make sure things at home are taken of."

"It's okay that you're not working right now," she exchanged. "Just keep working at the youth center and I think we'll be okay. Did you call Lenny back today?"

"Yes, I did," he started slowly as he got up. "He sounded different. We were just kids when we met but something seemed off about him. He seemed as if he was in a rush to get off the phone and right before I hung up, he apologized for what happened to me."

"For you joining the gang?"

"I think so. He said, '*I'm sorry for what he did to you*,' just as he was hanging up, and before I could say anything else, he was gone. He sounded sincere and

I'm not sure what he knows but I get a sense that he may need some help. He may be in trouble."

"See!" she threw her hands up. She rubbed her face nervously and sighed. "If he's in trouble, we don't need that. Please let him be and he'll find the help he needs."

"I don't know if it's that kind of trouble. He didn't ask me for anything besides some time to meet. I think I'm going to meet with him."

"How do you even know it's not that kind of trouble?" she questioned with conviction.

"I'm not sure. It sounded like he needed someone to listen to him. He just wants to meet in person."

She had concern painted all over her face and Oliver could tell her worry had resurfaced. "If you go, I'm afraid you're going to get sucked back in. I get that he needs help, but I don't want to lose you just to save him."

He wrapped his arms around her to comfort her.

I hate seeing her upset like this, he thought. *I know she wants to protect me, and I love her for that but some things I need to do.*

"If I go" he began in a whisper. "I very well *may* get sucked back in and it may undo everything you and Dr. Novak spent years helping me fix. I *may* leave with more questions than I have now which may torment me and keep me up at night. Most importantly, I *may* feel something seeing him again after all this time. I'm not sure what that feeling will be, but it leads me to one last question that I know I'll never answer if I decide not to meet with him… "What would've happened if we had met?"

Oliver saw he still had her attention, so he continued. "I need to do this. Trust me."

"I do. It's him I don't trust but if you think this is what you need to do, do it. I'm going to wash up."

With that, he found himself alone in the kitchen as he finished preparing dinner. He lowered the stove and sent Lenny a text message, which he knew his estranged friend had been waiting for.

Hey man – It's Oliver. Let's meet tomorrow - Come to the library at 42nd Street and Fifth Ave. I'll be there at 10 a.m.

Almost instantly after Oliver placed his phone down, he received a notification sound that his message was sent, then another that a message had been received.

Thank you, thank you! I'll be there at 10 a.m.

CHAPTER 5:

HOW COULD HE HAVE FALLEN SO LOW?

Oliver Burke

The next day, Oliver found himself sitting at a communal table on the 2nd floor of the New York Public Library. This location was public enough to provide him with witnesses, if needed, but also offered some privacy as he knew their conversation would shed light on some of the darkest parts of their shared past. Parts that he wanted answers to but had no interest in sharing with others.

As he sat and waited, Oliver's anxiety struck causing his palms to feverishly moisten and his forehead to perspire. As he looked around, he noticed there were people around, more than he expected, but how quiet it was—almost eerie.

Maybe this isn't private enough. Maybe I should have chosen something else.

It was now 10:15 a.m., which was fifteen minutes passed their agreed-upon time, and Oliver grew further anxious.

Where is he? Why would he tell me he'd be here at 10 a.m. and not show up? I knew I shouldn't have agreed to this. I should just leave. Amerie was right. This was a bad idea.

His impatience was now obvious, and he began to gather his belongings to leave. His eyes hardened and narrowed into slits as he packed his things. His muscles were clenched, and he shook his head in disappointment.

He played me. I need to block his number and just move on. No more calls, no more texts, no more voicemails.

At the moment he rose to his feet, Oliver noticed he'd caught the gaze of a man, who stood on the other side of the room and was now walking up to him. As the man approached, Oliver thought to himself.

Is that Lenny? Can't be – he looks so...old

The man had a subtle vigor in his approach, which reminded Oliver of the strut Lenny used to walk with. Although he still had a bit of swagger left, it was obvious he was in his declining years. He carried frailty in the way he moved which indicated his body also matched everything else. The man also had a scar underneath his lips, to the left side of his face, which Oliver didn't recall.

When the man finally arrived at the communal table, the two men stood and silently stared at each other. Oliver's frustration had now softened as he peered at this dowdy individual staring back at him. The man appeared as if he was no younger than seventy years old and carried several wrinkles that paired perfectly with his receding hairline. Although his body seemed debilitated and timeworn, Oliver could sense there was youth behind the man's appearance because of the glow in his eyes. He could tell the man was happy to be there with him.

Can't be - We should be around the same age. How does he look like this? He thought to himself as he stared into the man's seemingly sad, but luminescent, eyes and asked.

"Lenny?"

"Yes, Oliver – it's me. It's been a long time."

Oliver continued to stare back, as he searched for the right words. He could tell Lenny was looking for a hug but chose not to give in. He scanned Lenny's face and could see his bottom lip quivering and tears welled from the corner of his eyes. Behind the initial glow, he could see an emptiness behind Lenny's eyes and sensed they both were attempting to gather the right first words. Seconds later, Lenny finally found his.

"I'm sorry that it's taken me so long. I know I'm a little late. I couldn't find you and frankly, I don't move like I used to."

"What happened to you?" Oliver questioned. "You look so…"

"Old?" Lenny inserted, filling the space in Oliver's unfinished sentence. "Yeah, I know. Not everyone had access to the fountain of youth. Shit, I wish I had access to *any* of my youth." He cleared his throat and continued. "Look man, I know it's been a long time, and I—"

Oliver interrupted as the volume in his tone grew. "Lenny stop!" He saw others, including a young blond no older than Walter, look over so he lowered his voice back to a whisper. "You disappeared randomly when we were kids, and I didn't even know if you were still alive. Now you show up out of the blue and say, 'I know it's been a long time.' Where the hell were you and why did you want to meet?"

Lenny looked back and shook his head in understanding of Oliver's frustration. Although Oliver's voice rose to levels indicating he was angry, Lenny had no intentions of reciprocating this emotion. Oliver could see he was joyous to be there and watched as he simply sat and clasped his hands together. Lenny was almost on the verge of tears and continued.

"Oliver…I thought about this moment for a long time. I don't know what to say but I'm glad you came."

"Lenny…what do you want? How and why'd you find me?"

"Straight to the point I see. Look, I know you have questions and I hope to answer them all but want you to know that when I got back, I searched all of Brooklyn looking for anything that connected me to you. I went by the old foster house you used to live in and now it's a Starbucks. I went by the park to see if anyone remembered you and it was empty. I even went to the high school we used to go to but nothing. I can't believe how much things have changed. Most people I spoke with hadn't even heard of you besides one cop at this recreation center downtown."

Lenny pulled out a printed copy of the article Walter showed Oliver, unfolded it, and slid it in front of him. "I saw this article about someone named Oliver Burke who looked like the Oliver Mahlah I used to know back in the day and when I showed up to meet with him, I met the cop who works there. Officer Jefferson, I think his name was. He told me y'all were friends and you were helping take care of the center. That's so dope man. You used to be this badass orphan, now you're helping other kids. That's really great man—I'm proud of you. I told him we were friends also and he gave me your number. Then I called you and here we are. That's how I found you."

As he wrapped up, Lenny pulled out a cigarette and place it between his lips. Oliver saw his hands trembling and could sense this vice was in place to calm his nerves. Just as he went to light it, Oliver interjected.

"You can't smoke that here."

Lenny froze, looked around, and disapprovingly put the unused cigarette back into the breast pocket of his jacket. He looked over at the others also sitting at the communal table and saw them shaking their heads.

"Oliver—look man. I'm glad to see you. Remember how I used to beat your ass in basketball?"

"Lenny... why are we here? What do you want from me?" His voice started to rise and in that same moment, he once again connected eyes with the same young blond, who was now angrily packing her things to move tables. He lowered his tone back down to a mutter, turned back to Lenny, and leaned in as his friend continued.

"Okay, Oliver, I..."

Just at the same moment, Lenny was going to respond, his phone began to ring and when he looked at the caller ID, his eyes lit up. He used his index finger to indicate he needed a moment then picked up the call.

Oliver could tell this was a call his friend had been waiting for and simply sat silent, looking at his own phone for any missed messages. When he looked back up, he watched as Lenny's facial expression went from content and excited, to disappointed and despairing. When he hung up the phone, Lenny exhaled and continued.

"Look Oliver—I need to go to take care of something urgent right now, but can we meet again? Please? I should be back in a few days and promise to tell you everything. Please, man."

In normal fashion, Lenny had given him just enough information that he had to piece together his own conclusions based on the few clues shared. Oliver knew he still had several unanswered questions but felt he'd met his obligation to himself.

"I don't know, man. We met and I don't know if it's a great idea for us to meet again. What do you *really* want?"

Lenny's face drop and he sat in disbelief at the fact that he'd wasted their first meeting. He looked at Oliver with disappointment in his eyes.

"Please," he begged. "Please Oliver, I need this. There's so much I need to tell you."

Oliver could see desperation he'd never seen before in Lenny. He remembered his friend as a confident, social jubilee who had more swagger than the word.

He thought to himself, *how could he have fallen so low?*

He could sense the extent of Lenny's desperation and knew he still had questions that he needed answers to. He believed Lenny was prepared to stay at the library if it meant this would be their last encounter and didn't want that, so he agreed to another meeting.

"Okay, Lenny. We can meet again but next time, I need answers."

"And you'll get them. Thanks, man."

The two men stood and made their way towards the exit. As they walked, Oliver noticed Lenny trailing and looked back impatiently. He'd grown used to his own New York City haste and noticed the clear disparity between that and Lenny's sluggish mobility. What would have normally taken someone seconds to do took Lenny longer and Oliver was convinced something was wrong.

When they finally arrived at the library exit, Oliver extended his hand and Lenny looked at it with hesitation. He could tell Lenny wanted more but this was all he was willing to give at this moment, so the two men shook hands and went their separate ways.

As he made his way home, Oliver's mind fixated on Lenny's physical appearance. He thought about his frailty and concluded with one final thought which echoed in his mind.

Something's wrong.

CHAPTER 6:

TIME

Oliver Burke

As promised, Lenny did return a week later and contacted Oliver to arrange for their promised follow-up meeting. In his text, he joked about how he needed a few extra minutes to make his way over and asked for "no more libraries," which Oliver assumed was so he could smoke.

Sure Lenny — Let's meet by the north side of the lake in Central Park. I should be there by noon.

Perfect, Lenny replied almost instantly.

Lenny should have been roughly the same age as Oliver and he was still very curious as to why his estranged friend had aged so poorly, and before leaving the house for their meeting, Oliver searched WebMD for any information he could find. Sadly, his search resulted in several entries which made it difficult for him to choose just one. He knew that the only way he would know exactly what was going on was to ask and decided that he would add Lenny's health to his growing list of questions.

It was now early November, and the weather was still on the cusp of the fall/summer heat and winter chill, which made days outside enjoyable—especially after such a sizzling summer. Oliver had grown used to the heat because of his time in the graveyard and now welcomed every opportunity he could take to enjoy the cooler days.

*****

As agreed upon, Oliver did give Lenny extra time and when he arrived, he saw him sitting on a bench staring blankly at the lake. As he approached, Oliver examined Lenny's sleepy eyes and drooping cheeks. He looked intently into the face of this old man and struggled to find his best friend in this stranger. It was as if he was seeing him for the first time all over again.

When Oliver arrived at Lenny's location, he looked at his face with curiosity. His eyes first locked on the scar underneath Lenny's lips then he once again extended his hand in greeting. Instead, Lenny stood to his feet and went in for a hug—which Oliver reluctantly accepted. There were still so many questions on his mind, and he struggled to find his friend in the man who stood in front of him that day. He planned to take the same approach today, but once Lenny wrapped his arms around him, Oliver could feel how frail he'd become, and simply stood there.

In their embrace, Oliver felt the tension Lenny was carrying and noticed it begin to relax the longer he held him. He could sense a physical pain in Lenny's hold by how his muscles shook, and as time went on, he could tell how comforting their hug was for his friend.

Oliver wrapped his arms around Lenny and returned the embrace. For moments, the two of them stood there and held each other tighter and longer until Oliver could no longer hear the silence of Lenny's tears falling from his cheeks onto his shoulder.

"Thank you for meeting with me again," Lenny remarked wiping his face and clearing his throat. "Sorry again for the other day."

At that same moment that their bodies retracted, a young African American boy, no more than eight years old, walked up from the edge of the lake. He approached them, squeezing his shirt with both hands in awkwardness, looking with wide-eyed puzzlement, and sat beside the pair on the bench. He looked up at Lenny then traded glances to Oliver and back. Lenny turned his attention to his friend and smiled.

"Oliver, this is Sebastian. We call him Bastian or Bas. He's my grandson."

Oliver sat in shock. Another revelation that added to the already extensive list of questions he had in his mind. Lenny continued.

"Bas, meet my best friend in the whole world, Oliver," he extolled. "He's the one I told you about. Say hi."

Oliver still in shock stared at the young boy.

"Hi," Bastian remarked shortly and softly.

"Hello, Bas."

Bastian turned his attention away from Oliver and back to Lenny. "Grandpa, can I go feed the ducks?"

"Yeah, Bas but make sure I can see you and you can see me, okay?"

"Ok!"

As Bastian walked away, Lenny turned back to Oliver who still wore his surprise.

"Told you we had a lot to catch up about. Look, Oliver, I'm so sorry I disappeared all those years ago. I got in over my head and had to go away for a little bit. It wasn't how I pictured my life going but I guess that's the way things turn out for people like me."

Oliver continued to stare intently, waiting for the additional bombshell revelations he knew were coming, so Lenny continued when he was certain he had his attention.

"Since we saw each other last, a lot has happened to me. Things you wouldn't even believe."

Oliver looked over at Bastian and back at Lenny, which his friend took notice of.

"Yeah. Bas. He's mine. It's been a long thirty years but essentially, I had a daughter—Simone. Man, she was the prettiest thing ever and was smarter than most of these ivy league fools in their fancy uniforms and expensive education."

Oliver thought to himself, *was?*

Lenny's attention was unwavering. Oliver watched as he stared at others rowing on the lake and continued.

"That was Bastian's mother. She got mixed up with the wrong crowd at a young age and lost herself. I tried everything, man. Everything I could but it was never enough. Guess I always had a way of not being there for the people I cared about most. You know, kind of getting there too late type of thing."

Oliver could tell Lenny was struggling to talk about Simone and placed a hand on his feeble shoulder to show his support. Lenny gave him a wounded look and continued.

"She had Bastian when she was sixteen years old. Sixteen! She was just a child having a child and wasn't strong enough when she had him. She passed away on the hospital bed and just like that, my baby was gone. Thank God Bas came out okay but sometimes I think, her life was traded for his because I didn't deserve them both."

Lenny's voice began cracking and Oliver could sense he was struggling to talk about his deceased daughter. He felt embarrassed at his original anger as it began to subside.

"I'm so sorry, man…I didn't know."

"It's cool. Nothing we can do about it now but move on. Bastian is my responsibility and has been for the last seven years. I'd do anything for that boy including making sure he grows up in a caring and loving home like I did before I went away."

Lenny paused.

"It was never my choice to leave…"

"What?"

"It was never my choice to leave you, let alone stay away. You were my best friend, Oliver. My only friend really. When I heard what he did to you…"

He paused again and cleared his throat—holding back his tears.

"When I heard what Rahzmel did to you, that was the moment I realized how much of a mistake I made bringing you to the clubhouse that day when we were kids. You may not believe me, but I thought about that day and you, every day for the last three decades. How much different both of our lives may have been if we'd stayed in school like we were supposed to."

Oliver looked straight at Lenny and could tell there was a deep honesty behind his words. It was as if Lenny was in a confessional and Oliver was his priest tasked with clearing the emotional debt Lenny assumed he owed.

"Lenny…I can tell you're not doing okay. You were gone for all that time. What really happened to you in that time?"

By now, Oliver's anger had completely vanished, and he was left deeply worried for his friend. He watched as Lenny paused in his story and fought back the sudden rush of emotion that was beginning to overwhelm him. Although he didn't fully comprehend the extent of Lenny's pain, he continued to pat his friend's back to display his understanding of what he was going through.

"Lenny? You don't have to continue. I can tell this is hard for you."

"Talking about this is one of the hardest things I think I've ever had to do. Not because of what happened to me but because it took so long for me to find you and tell you all of this. I almost can't believe I'm here."

At that same moment, Lenny's voice began to once again crack so he paused. He closed his eyes, took a deep breath then cleared his throat again before continuing.

"Man...we would have done great things if we had the time. Imagine me and you...killin' it on the basketball court and getting all the girls when we were teenagers. Going to the same university on scholarships and moving next door to each other. We both would have found good women... *good women*," he emphasized with a smirk while keeping his gaze on the lake. "Who would've given us both tons of kids. I bet our kids would be best friends too, right? Like me and you? I bet they would've seen us and had to have been close."

Lenny finally turned his attention to Oliver and wiped the slow tear that began to form in the corner of his eye. His eyes were puffy, and Oliver knew his testimony was the beginning of a dark recount of their history.

"I was checking in on you all the time while I was away. Watching from a distance type of thing, you know? Although we were far away, I was still there trying to protect you. Listening to what was happening. Shit – I could barely protect myself but still wanted to make sure you were good."

"What do you mean?" Oliver questioned as Lenny used his hands to cover his face in shame.

"Oliver, the reason I disappeared was that I got jammed pretty badly. I thought it was going to be one of those in-and-out types of situations, but I was wrong. Next thing you know, and a lifetime later, I'm searching for you and here we are."

"Jammed-up?"

"Yeah, man. Rahzmel didn't look out for me like he did for you. I got a long story and I want you to hear it. I needed you to hear this story."

"That's what I came here for, Lenny," Oliver admitted. "Things were going so well with us and then you just disappeared. I was alone again. I wish we could've had all those things too, but you left man."

There was a pause. Lenny smiled and turned his attention to Bastian, then called over.

"Yo, Bas, you want to play at that park?" he screamed while pointing to the adjacent playground which was filled with children and their guardians.

"Yep!" he remarked walking over while wiping the dirt from his hands.

"All right man. Go play over there with the other kids. Be good. Don't kick anyone, don't pinch anyone, or we're leaving. Okay?"

"Okay," he responded running over in obedience.

After Bastian was gone, Lenny turned his attention back to the lake.

"You got time?" he asked.

"Yeah. It's 12:30 p.m."

Lenny smirked then slowly pulled out a medication subscription bottle, which Oliver could tell was a fresh refill. Lenny watched his friend's eyes follow the bottle till it disappeared back into the same pocket it came from.

Right as Lenny swallowed the pill, he looked Oliver in the eyes. "You got time, right?"

Oliver looked back in concern. *Why's he asking me about the time again?*

"Yeah, Lenny, I have time. Do you?"

Lenny gave another smirk at the question and reached into the same breast pocket of the jacket he was wearing during their previous visit. He grabbed a fresh pack of cigarettes, pulled one out, and lit it— quickly inhaling the smoke into his lungs and coughing furiously. Oliver patted him on the back to help him catch his breath which he responded to with a smile.

"Yeah… I got a little time."

Lenny smirked as he looked up at his friend. Oliver could see he was beaming in excitement and realized how important this moment was to his friend. When Lenny saw his smile, he cleared his throat and began.

PART II
FIVE STAGES OF GRIEF
(LENNY'S STORY)

CHAPTER 7:

LENOX AVE

Thirty-three Years Prior   *September 1984*

"Mr. McNair... Mr. McNair... are we boring you?" the young educator remarked in a manner absent of empathy.

Lenny slowly rose his head and he wiped his eyes to clear his sight. As his vision began to discern between his dream and reality, he noticed his teacher was standing over his desk with a look of impatience he'd become very familiar with. He knew there was no way this could be a dream.

"Sorry, long night of studying," he joked in hopes of catching a few laughs from the room. He was mostly successful except for the one laugh he was looking for—his teachers.

"I'm sure," the instructor badgered turning back to the board to continue. The class giggled just as hard at his teachers' reciprocation, which Lenny took notice of. He felt embarrassed and shook his head.

*****

Growing up in Harlem before moving to Brooklyn, Lenny had modeled his own life after two people. The first was the Harlem drug kingpin, Frank Lucas, who ran his empire with resolve and like a business. Lenny adored how Frank was respected on the streets but what he admired the most was how Frank incorporated his family in his dealings. Frank used to rub shoulders with elites within entertainment, politics, and even the criminal underworld, which reminded him closely of the second person he copied.

Rahzmel Davis was Lenny's older cousin, by blood, and was the only other person he held in the same regard as Frank. He venerated him because of how he'd become a big-time drug dealer in Brooklyn and how Rahzmel had taken care of him during his upbringing. There was roughly ten years in between them and although they didn't grow up together, they shared moments before and after Lenny moved from Harlem. Like Frank did for his own relatives, Rahzmel gave Lenny small opportunities to support his drug business, which Lenny grew to appreciate over time.

Although Lenny feared Rahzmel, like so many others, he also appreciated Rahzmel because of the challenges they both faced during their childhoods. They'd both survived the sins of their fathers and absences of their mothers, and as his life spiraled out of control, Rahzmel was there checking on Lenny— almost like the father he didn't have.

*****

As his teacher stood over his desk this day, Lenny thought back to Rahzmel and Frank and considered what approach they would have taken if they'd been the ones disrespected by this young educator.

Frank's loud and would probably pull out a gun and shoot him. That's too violent and I'm nothing like that. Nah. I need to be like Rahzmel. He's quieter and would probably sit there silent then strike back when the teacher's alone. I'm not violent like him either but maybe I can say or do something instead.

Although he thought to be more like his cousin, he also wished others, like his teacher, could see he was tough also and avoided antagonizing him. Rahzmel's presence alone carried a heavy weight to it in Brooklyn because of his long history. The kind that made others carefully calculate their tone and never question him.

He knew he couldn't take the approach of either Frank or Rahzmel, and instead, decided he needed to act or feared he'd lose the respect he assumed he had from his classmates. In an effort to blatantly defy his instructor's directive, he placed his head back down on his desk and began to drift back to sleep. Moments after he had fallen asleep, he heard his name being called again.

"Mr. McNair... do I have to repeat myself? You can't sleep in my class! Save that for when you're home in your cage," his teacher remarked giggling at his own comment.

"Yo, fuck outta here," Lenny shot back. "Dead ass, you better put some respect on my name."

"Put some respect on your name? What does that even mean?"

"Man forget you!"

"Well, *Lenny*—"

"It's Lenox to you, bitch" Lenny interrupted as he looked around the room for an ally to support his stand. He found no one.

His teacher smirked, ignored his comment, and continued.

"Well *Lenny*, if you don't have anything to contribute to the class for today, might as well leave.

Think you can spend the rest of the day in the principal's office. Goodbye."

"Whatever."

Lenny grabbed his baseball cap and his books then departed through the door—slamming it shut behind him.

This was his second time repeating the tenth grade at Roman Reade Public High School and because of that, he'd assumed he'd heard it all. He had no interest in sitting through another lecture about how he *won't amount to anything unless his attitude changed, blah... blah... blah.* Although he didn't want to disappoint his grandmother by being sent home from school again, he also knew he wouldn't accept his teacher's ridicule. Neither Frank nor Rahzmel would have tolerated it.

As he ambled through the halls aimlessly, Lenny noticed another African American teenage boy walking in the same direction. The kid was Lenny's height, had a dark Caesar haircut, and wore the same look of indifference that was painted all over his own face. Like himself, this kid wasn't dressed like most of the other students and Lenny assumed he also didn't *fit in,* so he approached.

"Yo, man, where you heading?"

"I got kicked out of class so I'm heading to the principal's office to try to explain myself," the teen responded suspiciously.

"Damn man...I got kicked out for falling asleep. I'm supposed to go to the principal's office too, but I really don't feel like gettin' another fuckin' lecture today. I swear this school finds any and every reason to remind me that I'm a failure. I really don't need to hear that today."

Lenny looked the mysterious teen up and down again then quickly pondered.

"I'm probably about to ditch school for the rest of the day."

The boy looked confused. "And go where?"

"I got this place outside of school that I like to hang at. When I want to leave school, I usually make some shit up so if they call my house, my grandmama doesn't get mad. I'll just say I was in the nurse's office or something. As long as you sign into school in the morning, they don't call home." Lenny's tone sounded like he was attempting to persuade the teen and himself. He looked down both ends of the long hallways shadily and extended a hand. "I'm Lenny by the way but my friends call me Lenox."

"Why do they call you that?" the boy responded as if it were a joke.

"Well, you ain't my friend so there's no reason for you to know," he replied as he laughed in amusement. "What's your name?"

"My name's Oliver.... But people call me.... Ummm... Oliver Mahlah."

"Ahhh the infamous Oliver. From Dunbar House, right? I've heard of you. Your name's causing a bit of noise in this school. I hear you move on your own time and don't really do the rules thing...like me."

"Ain't no better time than my own," replied Oliver boastfully.

"Ha! I feel you." Lenny looked down the hall again, this time he placed one hand on Oliver's shoulder and guided him around the corner, so they were out of sight. "Listen here, I'm about to connect with some friends outside of school. You want to join or nah?"

He watched as Oliver took a moment to ponder the invitation before responding. "Umm, sure. Why not?"

Lenny grinned back and jumped in excitement. He was eager to show his new friend the life he'd been accepted into.

*****

The two teens walked the streets of East New York and learned more about each other. Oliver shared details on Dunbar Home, which was a hostile group home he currently resided in located in Canarsie.

"It's tough, man. Everyone kind of does their own thing there but at any given moment, someone can snap and rob or attack you. I've been there for a while but still haven't gotten comfortable. Don't think I ever will."

Lenny knew how rough the Canarsie neighborhood of Brooklyn was and compared it to the hard-hitting neighborhood he grew up in back in Harlem.

"Yeah, I came up around Frank Lucas and 'em." He boasted. "My grandmama moved me out to Brooklyn to live with her cause it was getting too dangerous back in Harlem. Nothing I couldn't handle but you know how that goes. That's why they call me Lenox."

"Lenox?"

"Wait…you've never heard of Lenox Ave? You must've been living under a rock."

"Nope…never heard of it. Anyways, where are we going?" I never been to this side of town," Oliver remarked nervously as he attempted to look for familiarity on each street they passed.

"You scared? Don't worry, man, there's this clubhouse just around the corner from here. We can hang out there for a bit if you want."

"Whose clubhouse is it? They cool with me coming with you?"

"They cool as long as you cool, man. Don't be weird and you got nothing to worry about. Don't think many people are there anyway. We should be good."

"Cool."

Roughly twenty minutes later, the two teens arrived at a seemingly abandoned building on Flatlands Ave., which had barred windows, a large metal door, and a security camera pointed directly at the entrance. The building seemed empty, as Lenny had indicated, but there were several vehicles parked out front which included a black 1984 Range Rover that Lenny seemed to recognize.

Oh, man. Croc's truck is here. I thought the house would be empty. They're supposed to be out.

He grabbed Oliver's arm and was seconds away from turning around but when he looked over at his new friend, he saw curiosity in his stare.

I can't seem like a punk in front of him. Not after all that shit I was talking about earlier.

He forced a smile and proceeded up the steps and signaled his arrival by giving the metal door a special knock and waving to the camera pointing at them. He forced confidence with a smile to reassure Oliver that he'd been there hundreds of times before and this was just another visit.

Seconds later, a large dark-skinned individual dressed in all black opened the door and stared at the two teens. He held his gaze and exchanged glances with both. Lenny peered over at Oliver and noticed the curious look he carried during their commute was now gone and all that was left was a look of trepidation. He turned back to the large individual and proceeded to stare him down squarely in his eyes. The man stared back and for seconds, neither broke their gaze creating a tense moment Lenny could sense was making Oliver uncomfortable. The man didn't seem like an aggressor because he wanted to be. All he did was stand up straight and it was obvious he was not someone to be confronted about anything.

Suddenly the large man winked, and he and Lenny erupted in laughter which was followed by a special handshake displaying an obvious understanding.

"Who's ya friend?" questioned the man in his deep voice.

"He's cool, Croc. He's a friend from school. We both got kicked out, so I brought him with me. This is Oliver."

"You got kicked out *again,* lil man?" he emphasized with an accompanying shake of his head. "You know Rah doesn't like you skipping days at school."

"Well, more like I left… Is Rah here? I'll explain."

"Nah, he's out with the others but still…"

Thank God, Lenny thought to himself. He continued. "Well, this will be our secret, Croc. If Rah comes in before I leave, I'll explain what happened. If he doesn't come back while I'm here, then this will stay between the three of us. Please?"

"Ok, lil man," replied Croc as he chuckled in amusement. "You're lucky I like you. We got drinks in the back. Nice to meet you, Oliver. Go have fun."

When the pair entered, they walked down a long, dark hallway to the main room. The space was brightly lit and was filled with couches, tables, a pool table, a large refrigerator, and large television. On the table was a white powdery substance that Lenny had seen around haphazardly at the clubhouse before and a few small bags of marijuana. Two half-dressed black women were sitting on the couch watching TV and a third who entered one of the back rooms just as Lenny and Oliver had arrived. The third one who entered the back room was much older than the others and was fully dressed.

"What's up, Angela. How you?"

"I'm good, baby. How you?" she responded as she nodded her head in greeting, but no one saw her smile. Before she could even wait for Lenny's response, she disappeared into the room.

"I'm good…"

On one of the tables, Lenny saw a half-full bottle of Irish Whiskey and walked straight towards it, uncapped the top, and took a large gulp. As he swallowed the crimson liquid, he exhaled a sigh of relief indicating his pleasure then looked over at Oliver, who still seemed suspicious. He could tell he needed to help his new friend get comfortable and handed him the bottle, hoping he would also take a swig. Instead, he watched as Oliver stood there and stared at it with confusion.

"It's just whiskey, man. Take a sip."

Oliver switched his attention from Lenny back to the bottle. As he did so, Lenny watched as his new friend contemplated his decision. He could tell Oliver was weighing the cost of his pride against the offer and put on a devilish smile of encouragement. He'd placed

Oliver between a rock and a hard place and felt a certain level of excitement.

If he doesn't drink this, I don't think I can hang with him again. If he does, this is my boy!

Dutifully, Oliver proceeded to take a big gulp of the drink, just as he saw Lenny do. Suddenly, he was hit with a hacking cough which lasted for seconds before he regained control of himself. It was obvious to Lenny that he was a novice in this area.

"What was that? It burns," questioned Oliver as he attempted to clear his throat.

"Just a little whiskey man. I'm assuming you don't drink?" Lenny offered as he held back his laughter.

"Nah, not really. I usually just chill."

"Oh, so you smoke?"

"Not really. I try to just stay low."

"No better way of staying low than to get high," joked Lenny as he pulled out a pre-rolled joint from his pocket and searched for his lighter. "I'm about to toke right now. You can join if you want."

"Nah, man, I'm good. I should be getting home. The school probably called Dunbar House so you know, I should go deal with that."

"Okay, man. Maybe next time. Hopefully, your people don't go too hard on you, and I see you back at school soon."

"Yeah, hopefully."

Lenny watched as Oliver made his way back to the exit and then departed. He turned back and took another sip of whisky before sitting between the two other women on the couch.

"Y'all want to smoke this with me?"

"Nah, I'm good," one of the women responded turning her attention from Lenny back to the TV.

Lenny sat unimpressed and turned his attention back to the TV.

Roughly ten minutes later, Lenny heard the large metal door unlock and open, then watched as three men entered the room. Angela had come out of her room and walked up to kiss one of the men, who had thick braids, a full beard, and a mustache. The man had gloves on and through his peripherals, Lenny could see the mangled scars on both of his forearms. The man looked over and connected eyes with Lenny who quickly diverted his attention back to the television. Still looking through his peripherals, Lenny could see the man looking at his gold wristwatch and Lenny's heart sank.

"What's good Lenny?" the man questioned in his deep voice.

"Nothing, what's good with you, Rah?" He replied with downcast eyes.

"Same old. Just taking care of some things with Rio and Chino. You know."

The man looked down at his wristwatch again and stared with murderous intent. Then he continued.

"Lenny, why are you here?"

"Listen, Rah, my racist-ass teacher embarrassed me."

"So you decided to leave school and come here?" Lenny could hear the sarcasm in Rah's voice and sensed there was underlying anger that was growing in his questioning. He continued to divert his eyes as the man clicked his tongue and his questions continued. "Lenny, didn't I tell you last week to stay your ass in school?" His upper lip curled in a sneer.

"Yeah, Rah but-"

"But what?" He interjected loudly. "But your racist teacher made you sad, so you left school and came here? For what? To cry?"

"Nah, Rah." Lenny looked over at the two others who arrived with Rah and saw them holding back their laughter. He heard Rah's tone growing bolder and more direct and fearfully lowered his head.

"Don't look at Rio, Chino, or the fuckin' ground! Look at me when I tell you this for the last time. Don't leave your fuckin' school. What happens when you leave is they begin to ask questions about why you're gone and when they ask questions, they start looking for answers about where you went. Do you want their investigation to lead them here? To me?"

"Nah, Rah."

"So don't fuckin' leave school! I swear you don't listen. If you weren't my cousin, I wouldn't even let you come here. I don't need grandmama breathing down my neck. The last thing she needs is two failures in the family."

"I'm sorry, Rah."

"Go home Lenny and keep quiet. You got a big fuckin' mouth and can't be inviting all your little friends here. In this business, we need discretion, and you can't be bringing people I don't know."

Lenny felt an unconscious twitching of his fingers and he stared without blinking. *How does he know Oliver came? Angela must have said something.* His mouth slowly dropped open and he stood frozen.

"Ok, Rah. I know. I'm sorry."

"You sure you get it because I feel like we're always having this conversation?"

"Yeah, I get it."

"Ok. Go home. I'll call you for the next pick-up. Tell grandmama I said hi."

There was a pause and just before Lenny walked away, Rah placed a hand on his chest to stop him. "Hold up Lenny. Better yet, don't tell her anything. You didn't see me. Got it?"

"Got it, Rah."

Almost instantly, the kingpin's face softened, and he forced a smile, exposing his yellow teeth which came as a result of years of smoking and poor dental hygiene. He moved his hand from Lenny's chest and gripped his shoulder firmly before leaning in to continue in a whisper.

"Sorry I gotta be tough on you. I want all of this to be yours one day and I need to show the others I'm not playing favorites just 'cause you're my cousin. This way they'll respect you when you become the boss. Makes sense?"

"Yeah, Rah. It makes sense."

Just then, Rah released his grip and proceeded to the back room with Angela, and Lenny made his way to the exit. As he walked through the door, he looked over at Croc who silently apologized for the embarrassment.

Shooed away, Lenny felt useless. He was connected to his cousin by blood yet in most of their interactions since he'd arrived in Brooklyn, it felt like he was on opposite sides of every room from him. He felt estranged and knew he needed to do better.

Rah was usually the smartest person in any room he was in which Lenny aspired. Although his cousin's tough love approach sometimes came with some embarrassment, he would typically associate their relationship with the relationship Frank had with his family members. He loved Rahzmel and assumed he loved him back, but also feared him. At times, when the kingpin spoke with him, there was affection and safety. At other times, there was nothing but contempt in his voice akin to a parent redirecting their child from their occupied seat at the adults' dinner table back to the kids' table.

Rah's the biggest drug dealer in Brooklyn and he lets me help out. Why do I keep messing up with him? I can't disappoint him anymore.

CHAPTER 8:

I LOVE YOU MORE

Lenny McNair

By the time he'd arrived home that evening, Lenny saw his grandmother in the kitchen and went to greet her with a customary kiss on the cheek. She was frying some pork and making his favorite, savory mashed potatoes with the peel still lumped in. She'd always said that people could not make rational decisions on an empty stomach because their attention was always impartial and motivated by hunger pains. For that reason, the house was always clean and the fridge was always filled. A safe space.

Periodically, he'd come home sulking, after a long day of his teachers' intolerance or his cousin's overbearing nature and would go straight to his grandmother for a hug. Rarely were words ever said to initiate their embrace, which she usually assumed was normal, but to him, it was his unvoiced assurance everything would be okay. It was a space where the cruel names or raised voices the world applied to him didn't matter and he could simply be.

"Hi, grandmama. Smells good."

"Thank you, baby. How was school?"

"It was good," he lied. "Same old. My teacher was picking on me again."

"What did he say?" she responded while wiping her hands.

Lenny could tell she was ready to act on anything he shared next and loved her for her protection. When he was in her presence, he felt comfortable letting his guard down. She appreciated him just the way he was, and he loved her unconditionally.

"Nothing really, just the usual. I'm cool though."

"All right, baby. Go wash up and get ready for dinner. I made pork chops."

"Yes, ma'am. Oh yeah, I heard from Rah today. He told me to tell you hi."

She shook her head and then walked away without responding.

I don't know why she hates him so bad. He's not that bad.

*****

The next day, Lenny proceeded with his school day as instructed. He bounced from class to class and made it a point to do better. He decided that he had to dress the part to "fit in" and forwent his usual baseball cap and jeans for khakis and a white button-up. He'd already garnered enough of his cousins' verbal wrath to last him a lifetime and wanted nothing but his acceptance. By the end of the school day, as he made his way to his locker to grab his backpack used for his drug pick up's, Lenny replayed Rahzmel's instruction in his mind.

Shoot. Rah told me to not mention his name. I forgot. I hope grandmama doesn't mention anything to him. He shook his head at the thought of his failure. *I can't keep doing this. Why do I have such a big mouth?*

He knew he was an important piece of his cousin's drug empire and didn't want to do anything to jeopardize his role. He'd seen what happened to others who were exiled from Rahzmel's care and had no intention of becoming another name forgotten.

Man, I need to do better. I don't want to end up like that one young dealer Rah made swallow a whole pufferfish 'cause he was talking too much. He thought. *I wonder what happen to that guy.*

To adhere to his cousin's directive and avoid similar issues, he decided to be better at school, keep to himself, and avoid any unnecessary attention, even if it meant biting his tongue. Although he didn't have many friends at school, he had a way with words and simply wanted his voice to carry him through high school.

After the final bell rang that day, Lenny approached his teacher to apologize for sleeping in his class during the previous day's lesson. He knew this was one relationship he needed to mend in order to avoid further difficulty for skipping the principal's office after being told to go there for reprimand.

"I'm sorry for yesterday. I won't sleep in your class again," he offered with sincerity.

His teacher had seen this type of regret in Lenny before but still accepted the apology because it usually was followed by a period where Lenny paid more attention to what was being taught and showed more respect toward who was teaching it.

"Thank you."

Lenny proceeded towards the exit and just before he grabbed the door handle, he turned back to his teacher, who was in the process of erasing the blackboard, and blurted.

"Do you think I have a big mouth?"

His teacher looked over at Lenny with confusion and smiled at the obvious trick question.

"Yes, Lenny. You do."

Lenny smirked as he left the room. Although his teacher usually got on his nerves, he appreciated his straightforwardness and confirmation of what he already heard from his cousin. Rahzmel's words were already etched in his mind, but his teachers' confirmation gave him the reminder he needed to try to do better and keep quiet—a task easier said than done.

Moments before he exited the school through the double doors, he heard his name being called and looked around. He didn't have many people considered friends, or even acquaintances, at Roman Reade High School, which made this situation strange. When he turned around and looked up, he noticed it was one familiar face he was happy to see.

"Yo, man. Yo, Lenny!" blurted Oliver as he ran over. "What's good? I've been looking for you."

Lenny turned in surprise. There was something about Oliver that Lenny trusted. Maybe it was the familiarity of both of their situations. Maybe it was the way he dressed. Maybe it was even the way he spoke. Whatever it was, Lenny trusted it. Like him, Lenny could tell Oliver also didn't have many people he considered friends and knew they were like one and the same. Outcasted, carefree, and far from conspicuous.

"Sorry man, I been in class and stayed after to ask my teacher some questions. I wasn't sure when I'd see you again but I'm glad you're here."

"Wow, look at us! Little scholars in the making! I see you even dressed the part today," Oliver joked with an accompanying playful shove.

At that moment, one of the larger upperclassmen was running through the hall and accidentally shoved

Lenny and Oliver as he tried to squeeze past them. The three of them tumbled to the ground and Oliver quickly shot to his feet. Lenny watched as anger overtook Oliver's facial expression from his grounded position and his fists were balled. He saw as his new friend's face got tight and hot, and imagined the blood that was rushing at that moment. The upperclassman also had fury on his face and Lenny was sure an altercation was coming.

Oh no…

"Get the fuck outta the way," the upperclassman sneered straight at Oliver.

He then turned his attention to Lenny, who was in the process of getting to his feet, and when he saw who it was, his own face swiftly changed from anger to fear. There was terror in his eyes and raw panic in his voice as he realized whom he'd shoved.

"Oh, man. Ughh…my…my bad," he stuttered as he extended Lenny his shaking hand in assistance. "Sorry, I didn't see you guys. Please don't tell your cousin about this. It was an accident."

Lenny looked at Oliver, who now wore a muddled look, then turned back to the upperclassman. "Ok man. Go on. Get outta here. We're all good."

When the upperclassman disappeared around the corner, Lenny turned back to Oliver and continued.

"Sorry about that, man. These ballplayers gotta watch where they're going. But yeah… shortly after you left the clubhouse yesterday, Rah came by and found out I left school *again*. Let's just say, it wasn't pretty. Last week, he warned me about leaving school and when he found out I left school *again*, he yelled at me. Bad!"

"Damn man. The house aide, Ms. Janet, from Dunbar House, chewed me out last night when I got home too. The damn school called her and told her what happened in class, so I tried to be on my best behavior. Dunbar House is a beast but I'm not trying to get kicked out of anywhere else. Who is Rah to you anyway? Why did he yell at you?"

At that moment, Lenny realized Oliver hadn't met his cousin during their visit and attempted to backtrack his remarks in hopes of following Rahzmel's directive to *keep quiet*.

"He's no one man. Forget I even mentioned his name. Listen … I gotta get out of here. I'll see you in school tomorrow?"

"Sure."

"All right. You play ball, right? Basketball?"

"Yep - I'm probably better than you too," Oliver replied with a lighthearted shove.

"Yeah right! After school tomorrow, let's head to the park and ball. Put your words to action."

"Yeah, let's do it."

The boys shook hands and went their separate ways.

In normal fashion, after leaving Oliver at the school exit that afternoon, Lenny made his way to complete his usual drug run for Rahzmel. This day was cooler for that period of the year and the teen could see the toll it was taking on the street hustlers. He watched as most insulated themselves within huddled groups of four or five to keep warm or freestyle battle rapped to prove who was best of them all. He would also catch a few popping in and out of local corner stores to purchase a snack, which he believed was partially influenced by their hunger, but mostly influenced by their need to escape the cold. He knew he couldn't bear to operate in their capacity and felt gratitude for his minor role within Rahzmels' operation. As he walked, he thought more about that role and all the possibilities.

I know one day Rah's going to let me take over. He tells me all the time. Even though he doesn't let me hang with them now, he says he's protecting me and preparing me. I know he's waiting for me to step up at the right time. Just like Frank did for his cousins. I just need to do my time and wait my turn.

Once he arrived in the Brooklyn Heights neighborhood, he looked around in glee. He thought back to one of his first visits to the territory controlled by the Japanese crew and how it had ended with Rahzmel taking him for some dim sum, which was followed by a massage in the back room of one of the salons.

That was the best massage ever, he thought and giggled. *She made me feel like a man. I need to ask Rah to take me back there some time. He really hooked it up.*

Once the pick-up was completed, Lenny made his way back to the clubhouse to drop off the money, as he'd done countless times before. He was excited for his cousin to see that he was still supporting his aspirations and hoped he would soon realize how important Lenny was to their success.

As he walked through the streets, an unusual level of paranoia washed over him, and he began trembling at the thought that he was being followed. He regularly looked over his shoulder—expecting to see someone and gained butterflies in his stomach at each step. The hairs on the back of his neck were standing up and with his sweaty palms, he felt goosebumps on his arm. He felt his inner voice tell him to run and after stopping to look around, he burst into a sprint.

As he ran, Lenny continued to peer around, expecting to see someone chasing him, but there was no one. His breaths were rapid, and he began to feel dizzy so he slowed down until he was two blocks from where he started running. He stared at others with wide-eyed puzzlement and did not see anyone stare back.

Maybe it's all in my head. I just need to get home.

He had not felt this way before and assumed it may have come from him being in a neighborhood outside of his own or his yearning to not disappoint his cousin, so he disregarded this and continued into the subway.

While commuting back to East New York, Lenny now noticed an unusually high number of drunks riding with him on the subway. He was used to traveling all over town with transients but today felt different. Most had their bottles out in the open, which he assumed was attributed to their lowered inhibitions or was a show of their disregard for the law.

Seeing this also reminded him of his father, Joe, whom he left back in Harlem when he moved in with his grandmother. Lenny still held resentment towards Joe for the way he treated him and shook his head at the similarities in their behavior. Joe was a selfish man who did just enough to almost destroy Lenny's developmental years. Although Lenny felt mostly indifferent towards him, he was happy that Joe's failures as a man, and father, brought him closure to his mother—Lenny's grandmother.

Lenny recalled Joe always being *around* when he was growing up but was never really *present*. In the moments that he was *around*, he was usually inebriated, and Lenny now only remembered the slur in his speech that came when he was drunk. He remembered how his father held his flask more than his own child and in the times he did hold him, it always felt foreign to him. As if Joe were counting down the seconds to release him from his grip and pick up his bottle. He couldn't remember the man sober.

In addition to their grandmama, Joe's failures also brought Lenny closer to Rahzmel, who used to pass by every now and then claiming to "check on them." He recalled the joy he used to feel when Rahzmel would come by because he always had the freshest clothes on, coolest gadgets, and always left Lenny with a little spending money, which he used to say was to "*help get us to God.*" Joe was always just as excited for Rahzmels' visits and Lenny cringed at the thought of his father's elation.

That bastard.

He felt himself growing upset and quickly diverted his attention back to his commute. He wasn't sure what it was about this day that brought the drunks all out in the open, but he disregarded it and made his way back.

When he arrived at the clubhouse, Lenny emptied the bag full of money into a container, then excitedly looked around for confirmation that he'd done well. Unfortunately, no one was home to greet him, so he decided to wait.

Damn, Rah's not here. I was hoping he would see me bring the money in. Need to make up for skipping school. Maybe I'll see him tomorrow.

Lenny continued to wait for another twenty minutes hoping he would at least catch someone who could pass along his accomplishment to Rahzmel, but no one came. He knew he had to go home in order to maintain appearances in front of his grandmother and left in disappointment.

Guess I'll catch them next time.

*****

"Hi, grandmama."

"Hi, baby," she exchanged with a kiss as Lenny returned home that evening. "How was school?"

"It was good. It was weird, on my way home, there were a bunch of people getting high and drunk on the streets and the trains. I don't think it's St. Patrick's Day or nothin' like that. I wonder what's going on."

Lenny's grandmother paused and put the spatula down. "It's a disease, baby. Just like your father had. It makes people do things they wouldn't normally do."

"Like what Daddy did to Mama?"

"Yes – your father wasn't raised like that. He lost his way at some point because of the disease. That's what made him beat up on you and your mama."

Lenny sat and watched as his grandmother thought about her only son. Although he didn't want to leave Harlem, he recalled conversations they had early on about how important it was to not only separate him from their small one-bedroom apartment but also from the city of Harlem which, at that time, was plagued with drugs and violence. She knew if she left him in Harlem, she would have sentenced him to a prison of his environment—which in many cases meant: jail, teenage pregnancy, or death.

Lenny continued.

"I don't know if I ever said it but thank you for letting me come live with you, grandmama."

"Lenny, you never need to thank me. Ever. I'm your grandmama and I love you. I raised your father better than that and I'd be damned if I left you in that house with him and those bottles. He's getting the care he needs so that's what matters. You're my responsibility now and I'll always watch over you. One day we'll get out of Brooklyn and get a small cottage in a good neighborhood. Okay?"

"Okay, grandmama. I love you."

"I love you more. Go wash up then we'll eat."

Just as Lenny began to make his way out of the room he stopped and turned back.

"Grandmama… I know you don't get along with Rah, well, because of the things he's into but do you think you'll ever forgive him?"

"Lenny, why are you asking me that?"

Lenny squeezed his backpack straps nervously and stared as his grandmother did not blink.

"Well looking at the drunks today made me think about it. What Daddy did to Mama. Rah used to be good. He used to look out for me when I lived in Harlem but since you kicked him out, maybe he lost his way too?"

"All I'm gonna say about it is whatever business your cousin's in, is no business of mine. People like him aren't good for people like your father. I can't forgive him. He needs to forgive himself first and that's all I'm gonna say about that. Don't bring that boy's name up in this house again. Okay? Now go wash up."

"Yes, ma'am."

CHAPTER 9:

THE BOY WHO LOST HIS HALO

Lenny McNair

Over the course of the next few weeks, Lenny continued with his good behavior at school and his daily pick-ups throughout Brooklyn. He felt his role within Rahzmel's organization growing and was thrilled to continue working towards his position as the kingpin's successor—a dream his cousin slowly began to regularly entice him with.

In this same period, Lenny had also grown very close to Oliver. They'd become fast best friends in a matter of months and Lenny was thrilled that he'd finally found someone else like him. He sensed an emptiness in Oliver that ran parallel to his own and connected deeply with him. The two of them shared various details of their lives, went to battle with others on the basketball court, and confided in each other over the various hardships in both of their lives. Oliver shared details of his arduous journey through the foster care program and Lenny shared details of the various contrast between Harlem to Brooklyn.

"My dad was an alcoholic and used to beat on my mama. He used to come home drunk every night and would find the smallest things to go at my mama for. One day, he took it too far and we fought. He got sent away and I had to leave. My grandmama says it's a disease, and he's getting help, but I have no mercy for him. I watched him beat on my mama every day and now he's dead to me. My grandmama took me in and has been taking care of me since. Besides my dad's alcoholism, I barely remember life before my grandmama. Truth be told, most of my childhood memories are with her."

Oliver stared. "I wish I had someone like that."

*****

One afternoon, Lenny was sitting outside during recess when two of the leaders from one of the partnering organizations pulled upon him in the schoolyard. He hadn't seen them on this side of town and grew worried.

"Lenny… we were in town and decided to drop off today's pick-up. Saves you a trip. Even threw in a little extra. Hope that's okay?"

"I thought I was just picking up money. This looks like more than just money," he remarked peering into the bag nervously.

Lenny could see the man had haste to him and seemed like he was in a rush.

"Do you want it or not?" The man remarked impatiently in his thick Irish accent as he looked around.

Lenny did not want to disrupt Rahzmel's business plans, nor did he want word of his defiance to make its way back to the kingpin, so he reluctantly agreed and took the bag. "Yes, that should be fine. I'll take it back to Rah. Should be fine."

Just then, the Buick sped away just as quick as it arrived. Unfortunately, Lenny still had the rest of his school day left and placed the bag into his backpack with the rest of his books.

By the time school had ended, Lenny began making his way to the clubhouse to deliver the goods to his cousin.

So glad they dropped off the money. Means I can go to the basketball court early and me and Oliver can bust some ass on the court.

During his commute, he began to once again feel as if he were being followed and grew anxious. He checked over his shoulder often and by the time he'd arrived at the subway platform and looked around, he was sure he was being followed.

I think I've seen that man with glasses before. Shit, I don't remember from where, but I recognize him. Gotta be careful. I can't go to the clubhouse. I need to go home. I'll drop the bag off somewhere and pick it up later. Rah will have to understand.

By the time he'd gotten off the subway, the same trepidation from before had arrived. *Wait yeah, I think that guy is following me,* he thought as he avoided eye contact. *What the hell's going on? This can't be the local police. Rahzmel owns them all.*

He then noticed an unmarked police cruiser trailing him in the direction of his grandmother's home. The car followed as he left the subway platform and made his way up Foster Ave. Rahzmel had shown him how to identify regular Chevys apart from the unmarked Impala's the police department had used, and this one was as clear as day. Every street he turned—the car turned until they both arrived at his grandmother's house. Just as he went to cross the street, the blue and red lights inside the dashboard shot on and Lenny froze in the middle of the road. When he looked around, he noticed there were several other unmarked police cruisers that also now had their lights on.

Oh shit. I really hope these cops are on Rah's payroll.

"Lenny McNair?" one of the plainclothes officers questioned as he approached while quickly flashing his badge.

"Yes?" Lenny froze in response. His eyes were wild with worry as he took a step back.

The officer placed his hand on top of the holster on the right him and approached slowly. "What's in the bag, son?"

"Nothing," Lenny shot back as he watched other officers also approaching from various directions around. Just then, his grandmother opened the front door and Lenny's eyes connected with hers.

"Lenny, what's going on?" she frantically screamed from the porch steps.

"Nothing, grandmama. Stay there. It's a mistake. I think they're mistaking me for someone else. Go back inside."

One of the officers saw her approaching and motioned towards the front of the house steps in case she decided to intervene.

"Son, what's in the bag?" the same cop questioned as he grew closer to Lenny. His tone grew louder and as Lenny scanned the scene, he noticed the other officers also had their hands on their holsters. He began to worry.

"I said nothing, sir! I'm just trynna' get home. I live right there see. That's my grandmama."

Wait...I don't think they're with Rah. Something seems wrong, he thought.

Rahzmel's cardinal rule of thumb rang in his mind as he stood there frozen. *If the police ever question you, don't mention anything about the crew.*

Lenny knew he had ¼ pound of cocaine in his bag, which he'd received from the Irish crew earlier that day, and feared there would be no way he could talk his way out of being caught. He decided he needed to act and swiftly bolted down the street towards the intersection. As he motioned, he could hear his grandmother yelling his name in the distance. "Lenny! Stop!"

He barely got 15 feet before one of the officers tackled him to the ground and ripped the bag off his back. His chest was down to the ground and the officer used his knee to hold Lenny down as they patted him for any weapons. He fought through their hold until they were able to restrain his hands behind his back.

"Give me your cuffs," one of the officers demanded from another as he attempted to control Lenny, who was still fighting to free himself.

"Please, let me go. I didn't do anything!"

The officer tore the bag open and smiled when he found the money and cocaine.

"Lenny McNair, you're under arrest for possession of a controlled substance. You have the right to remain silent. Anything you say can and will be used against you in a court of law. You have the right to an attorney. If you cannot afford an attorney, one will be provided for you. Do you understand the rights, I've just read to you?"

"Please let me go. This is all just a mistake."

The cop disregarded Lenny's plea and lifted him from the group. He placed the teen in the back of one of the cars and slammed the door shut. They drove away and from the back of the police cruiser, Lenny watched as the tears fell from his grandmother's face. He continued to stare until he could no longer see anything but a figure in the distance then turned back to the officers.

"Y'all do know whom I'm connected with, right?"

The officers didn't respond and drove off in silence.

*****

On Monday, November 5th, Lenny's arraignment was scheduled. As he entered the courtroom, he saw his grandmother sitting in the first row. Her eyes were red and puffy; as she looked at Lenny new tears started to form. Lenny saw this and dropped his head in shame.

How could I be so dumb?

His eyes quickly scanned the rest of the room and while he didn't tell Oliver about his arraignment, he was surprised, he did not see Rahzmel, Croc, or any of the others. He continued forward to approach the defendants' table.

Where are they? Where's Rahzmel?

By the time Lenny had been seated, he slowly turned back once again to search for a friend in the room and when he confirmed he was alone, he connected eyes with his grandmother and silently mouthed his deep regret.

"I'm so sorry. I love you."

Just before the judge began, a mystery woman, seated in the front row just behind Lenny, coughed loudly until she had his attention. She had an impassive look on her face and the first thing Lenny noticed was her permed hair, expensive shoes, and a light coat of makeup. She was dark-skinned – but not too much in Lenny's estimation. To him, she was beautiful and closely resembled the others Angela kept around the clubhouse. She was directly behind where he sat, and her palpable gesture caught his attention causing him to turn around and look over. When they connected eyes, she placed her index finger over her lips to subtly gesture for Lenny to remain silent. He sat further confused but slightly more hopeful.

I think Rah sent her. Yeah, he must have! He's probably going to get me out like he got Rio's sentence shortened back in the day. Yeah! You couldn't tell Rio nothin' after that!

He once again craned his neck and scanned the audience in hopes of seeing someone, but quickly turned back around in satisfaction. *I knew Rah wouldn't leave me here! This judge is probably in his pocket also. I just need to take what they give me and Rah will handle it. I know he will.*

As the public defender delivered his case, Lenny instinctively continued to interrupt and demand his innocence. They portrayed him as a drug dealer but to him, he was just in the wrong place at the wrong time. Every time the prosecutor shot back, he looked at his grandmother and then rescanned the room.

"Lenny sit down!" she yelled in embarrassment.

His public defender had on an ill-fitted suit and dilapidated shoes, and Lenny could sense he wasn't as comfortable as the prosecutor seemed. He had wide-eyed enthusiasm that only came from new public servants and ended every statement in a tone that sounded as if there was a question mark. Lenny looked into his brown eyes, which sat behind thick glasses and pudgy cheeks, and watched as he fought for his innocence.

"My client did not know what was in the bag. He was carrying it for a friend but cannot remember his name. We're requesting immediate dismissal of the charges."

That's it? Lenny thought in disbelief as he looked at the prosecutor who saw the look of incredulity painted all over his face.

The judge looked at them both then turned to the prosecutor who demanded a five-year sentence for the role he believed Lenny played in a bigger operation.

Five years? Lenny thought. *That's a long time. I think Rio got five years too and he was out and a few months. I think I'll be okay too.*

"This young man's clearly involved in something and if we let him back onto the streets, it will more than likely result in more drug addicts roaming the same streets with *our* children, *our* sidewalks continuing down a path where residents cannot even walk their pets without seeing an overdose or a dead body, and worst of all, more children, like this young man, who are also convinced they will one day be the next *king*." He looked over at Lenny with eyes that pierced straight through him. "What they don't tell you about this game is the lives it cost to get there, young man."

Lenny's heart sank at the prosecutor's verbal assault. The teen watched as he traded glances between the defendants' table and the judge until he made his final remarks.

"Your honor, I'm requesting a full five-year sentence to protect this young man from continuing on this downward spiral he clearly has no idea he's already on." He then peered into his manilla folder filled with notes and turned back to the judge. "Additionally, apparently this young man made a claim to the arresting officers questioning if they 'know who he's connected to.' This doesn't sound like the claim of an innocent man, your honor."

Lenny knew his big mouth would one day get him in trouble and was disappointed at the fact that the day had finally come.

Shit, why couldn't I just keep quiet?" He thought as his head dropped. *Rah's been telling me to keep quiet. Why couldn't I listen? He's right. I need to do better.*

The prosecutor then turned to Lenny and made one final plea.

"Young man. I can tell you don't want to be here, but you are here. I'm sure you have family and friends who are waiting for you back home. Unfortunately, you're not going home today."

Lenny's heart sank as the prosecutor once again traded glances between the public defender and judge. He still wore confidence in his look and smirked before turning back to Lenny and continuing. "I'm *only* requesting five years because I see so much potential in you but should really be requesting twenty years for the crime. We can make this easy or hard. I suggest we make it easy for both of us and your family back home." He then looked at the public defender who looked intrigued by the offer.

"How about it, huh? Take the five years or we can drag this out."

Lenny looked on as the public defender's face turned bright. He then looked at his grandmother and could tell she was still trying to make sense of everything being said. The prosecutor spoke fast; faster than he'd seen anyone talk, and he could tell his grandmama was having a difficult time keeping up.

I don't want to put her through a long process. I should just take the deal since I know Rah will get me out.

Before the public defender had a chance to deliberate with his client, Lenny interjected.

"I'll take it. I'll take the five years."

Both the prosecutor and judge looked at Lenny in surprise before the judge turned to the public defender.

"Is this your decision?"

The public defender looked at Lenny in surprise and before he could question Lenny on his decision, he watched as the teen shook his head in agreement.

"Yes, your honor," he replied with confusion as he looked at Lenny and then back to the judge. "My client apparently pleads guilty."

The judge quickly slammed his gavel, as if his decision was made hours ago, and the prosecutor jumped in excitement. He turned around to slap hands with others with him then returned his composure. The judge disregarded this and continued.

"This is highly unusual but nice to know we don't need to drag this out. Mr. McNair, I sentence you to five years in the juvenile detention wing of Port Authority Correction Center (PACC), for criminal possession of a controlled substance with an intent to distribute. Best of luck, young man. For your sake, I hope you are aware of what's happening."

When the judge slammed his gavel, Lenny broke down crying hysterically. He could barely speak and turned around to see his grandmother's face also painted with tears. As the officers placed the handcuffs back on his wrists, he finally found a voice and cried out. "Grandmama, I'm so sorry!" He remarked, numb with contempt and helplessness.

As he was carted off, Lenny scanned the room for one last time and once again connected eyes with the same mysterious woman in the front row. She made the same gesture less subtly and at that moment, he knew exactly what she was there for. She was sent by

Rahzmel and was tasked with ensuring Lenny was still practicing their code of silence. He knew how omerta worked and had no plans of turning on his cousin. He knew his cousin's threats came with verbal consequences but always carried the latent menace of something more severe.

Rah sent her. I hope he knows he has nothing to worry about and I won't snitch. Right?

He disappeared behind the courthouse door and cringed as the door slammed shut behind him.

CHAPTER 10:

PLEASE...STOP

Lenny McNair

When he arrived at Port Authority Corrections Center that morning, Lenny was taken to the main check-in desk where he was told they would start the extensive intake process he'd only seen on television. He stood shaking in fear as he slowly motioned forward towards the desk. He connected eyes with the guard who sat unamused and simply asked for Lenny to confirm the information they had. He could tell the guard had gone through this process countless times before and knew he was just another young black face about to be added to a judicial system built to hold murders, rapists, and other violent offenders. He could barely believe it.

"Name?"

"Ummm... Lenny... Lenny McNair."

"Date of birth?"

"July 7th, 1969"

"Okay...proceed."

He was quickly ambled through a series of procedures to check into the facility which included: fingerprinting, a complete body review to search for any gang-related tattoos or scars, and pictures. Once completed, a physical examination was performed by one of the male prison doctors who checked his mental and physical status. Lenny was registered at 175lbs, which was heavier than many of the other teenage male inmates but nothing that brought concern to the intake physician. He passed his exam and proceeded to the next steps.

As he walked out of the room, Lenny grew further worried at the fact that each step he took through the check-in process was one step further from his freedom. *This can't be happening.*

Next, his head was shaved clean, and he was forced into a communal shower with several other teenage inmates who were also arriving for their prison stints. When he quickly looked around, he could see a few of them had scars, bruises, and tattoos all over their bodies which was his confirmation they were not the same.

I'm not a gangster. Why did they place me here with these guys?

As the cool water fell on top of his newly shaved head, Lenny struggled at the thought of his current predicament. He wiped the tears that formed and stood motionless for minutes before the guard brashly pounded his baton against the wall to hurry him. As he thought about his cousin's lack of outreach, Lenny grew slightly worried but held back his tears around the others.

Where Rah? He should have had me out by now.

Once the shower was completed, Lenny stood in his underwear behind several other inmates also waiting for something at the end of the long line. He wasn't sure exactly what they were waiting for but knew between him and the end was roughly twelve inmates, most of whom wore their pride, fear, or anger on their faces like badges of honor. He continued forward until he was at the front of the line.

Once the door opened and the inmate in front of him was forced into the room, he saw exactly what was going on and looked back. Behind him were only two other inmates and a few guards looking on as if they'd seen this process hundreds of times before. He knew what came next and swallowed the heavy ball sitting in the back of his throat.

Moments later, the door shot open and one of the guards grabbed his shoulder to force him through until he heard the heavy metal door slam shut behind him.

"Stand on the stickers, drop your draws and turn around to face the wall, inmate," one of the guards commanded in a deep, arrogant voice that lacked compassion.

I can't believe I'm here. I can't believe this shit.

He followed the guards' command and lowered his underwear until they sat atop of his ankles and stared for further direction.

"Turn around and put your hands on the wall at 10 and 2"

"Yes, sir," Lenny replied scarily, and his voice shook.

"Did I say you should say a fuckin' word, inmate? Shut up and just do as I tell you. That's it. I don't want to hear a sound."

Lenny placed his hands on the wall where there were stickers indicating correct placement.

"Cough three times."

He did as instructed.

"Now take two steps back and crouch down like you're taking a shit."

Lenny looked back assuming it was a joke and connected eyes with the head guard who was a tall, white man with tattoo sleeves that stretched from his fingers up to his neck, a big beard, and an even larger belly that hung over his belt. He quickly read the name tag and shot his attention back to the wall in front of him. As he looked away, he could feel his face turning red. He felt a heaviness in his eyes as his tears urged his pupils to let them fall but knew he couldn't let them. He squeezed them shut and shook as he heard the guards' deep voice continue.

"Inmate... did I tell you to turn around? Look forward and crouch the fuck over."

Lenny slowly followed the command and just as he wrapped up his third cough, he began to slowly come back up.

"Hold up inmate, did I say you should come up?" The guard got up from his seat and slowly made his way to where Lenny was crouching. He got so close, that Lenny could smell the stale cigarettes and felt the guards' body heat radiating in the little space between them. The bearded guard placed his heavy hand on Lenny's shoulder and whispered. "Crouch back down and give me three new coughs. Real coughs not those pussy shits you just gave. Cough like you're trynna' vomit the drugs you probably took before you got here. I can help you cough if you need," he threatened.

Lenny did as instructed and when he finished, he waited for confirmation to rise. He again stood silent and looked at the wall in front of him while he waited for his consent before motioning to the door to depart. Once he'd finally received it, he turned to exit and walked through the door for his uniform. He was then carted to the bank of available payphones, which were mostly occupied by the others he arrived with. He stood tensely until a phone freed up.

He was instructed that he had two minutes for a call and rushed to the available payphone. He attempted to contact his grandmother but was unsuccessful.

C'mon, grandmama. Please pick up.

He tried several times and when she did not pick up, he decided to leave her a voicemail instead.

"Hi, grandmama. It's me, Lenny. I know you're probably really mad right now but want to say I'm okay. This is all just a big mistake and I promise I'll be out of here soon. I need to go now but I love you and hope to see you soon. I love you."

The guards then escorted the new cohort of inmates into the main building which was a short walking distance from the processing facility. Both buildings were connected by a long hallway that had no windows—just flickering lights, limited ventilation, and a stale smell of sweat, which Lenny quickly noticed. On one end of their group stood the burly guard who harassed Lenny during his processing. He shepherded the group from the front with a conviction that Lenny did not see in the other guards.

I don't want to get on his bad side again.

In the back of the group, two smaller guards were trailing who walked in a manner as if they too were being ambled. There was a clear distinction that showed who was in charge and Lenny could tell the other guards knew it too. He thought back to the name he read on the guard's name tag and motioned forward.

Kellerman...

As the group proceeded further into the cold facility, Lenny observed the same trepidation on the faces of the other fresh batch of inmates and grew further nervous. Fear gripped him and his lips trembled. Every bolted door behind them was one additional hurdle between Lenny and his freedom, and he grew extremely cornered at his new reality.

I don't think I can do this. I don't think I can do this. I don't think I can do this.

Prior to them delivering the inmates to their cells, the guards made one stop at the chow hall to demonstrate where the power stood. It was chow time, which had the hall mostly filled with teenage inmates and guards. Once the lead guard entered with the group, the room went silent, and most heads simultaneously turned in their direction. The lead guard gleamed with pride as he looked around the room to ensure he had everyone's attention. Lenny watched as most inmates in the chow hall hid their fear and instinctively wore relief on their faces instead. This new cohort of inmates meant attention was on them, even if just a moment. The existing inmates were relieved that for the moment, they were spared.

The lead guard didn't say a word and silently paraded their group around the hall twice, ensuring every inmate had an opportunity to see the fresh meat that had arrived. Although Lenny could tell most of the others were oblivious to this act, he knew exactly why they were there. It was a power-play he'd only seen done one time before—with Rahzmel.

As he walked, Lenny passed several inmates, much younger than him from what he could tell, gazing impassively at their trays of food. Most simply wore blank stares on their faces, while there were a few who Lenny could tell had been there a while. He sensed they'd already given up any hope and innocence, as a trade-off for their acceptance into the prison, and grew worrisome for his own fate.

Just before they left the hall, another guard approached the lead guard and whispered something in his ear, then pointed back at Lenny and another inmate. Lenny stood in shock at the fact that he'd already garnered the attention of the guards twice and feared what their conversation was about.

What's going on? What did I do?

The face of the lead guard quickly changed, and he nodded his head in agreement watching as his colleague approached Lenny. The guard pulled the two teens from the line and shoved them to move forward.

"Inmates… let's go."

"Where are we going?" Lenny questioned suspiciously. "I didn't do anything."

"They want to see you in the infirmary."

"Infirmary? What's that?" the other inmate questioned looking at Lenny and then back to the guard.

"It's the prisons doctor's office. It's a normal checkup. C'mon."

"Wait…I already had my check-up this morning. I thought that was the doctor. Why do they want to see us again?"

"Just follow me. I don't have more information besides that."

The three men motioned through a door on the other end of the chow hall and as they walked, Lenny could see the discomfort in the other inmates' body language. He was fidgeting and looking around quickly in a manner that made Lenny think he knew something bad was coming. They proceeded through a series of hallways, which felt like a maze until they reached a large red metal door.

"Open gate three," the guard remarked as he looked up into the camera facing the door. He used his baton to direct the inmates through the entrance and stood there as they walked through. Lenny sauntered through first and was followed by the other inmate. He looked down the poorly lit hallway, with doors ajar on both ends, and slowly proceeded forward. His shaking hands were still bound, and he assumed they were still being escorted until he heard the large metal door close behind him. When he looked, Lenny realized the guard had disappeared behind the door and it was now just him and the other inmate.

Like Lenny, the other inmate hadn't yet received a number on his uniform because of an apparent "technical issue" during processing which he now believed may have been intentional. He couldn't tell where this inmate was from but assumed he was Irish because of his auburn-colored hair which matched the Irish men Lenny had met in Brooklyn. Before he could say anything to the inmate, he saw a yellow liquid forming around his feet and his body was shaking. The inmate stood in the pool of his own piss, and it was now obvious to Lenny that something was wrong. He was frightened and the same fear began to assail Lenny. The inmate was staring down the hall and when Lenny turned around, he realized they'd been set up.

Wait… what's going on?

Three beefy-looking inmates entered quietly and slowly approached the two pinned-down teens. The three teens looked much older than Lenny and he knew exactly what their intentions were as he watched them wrap t-shirts around their hands like boxing gloves. Fear gripped him tightly as they approached and when he looked over at the other inmate who he'd arrived with, he saw he was now crouched in the corner sitting in a pool of his tears and urine.

I'm by myself and they're here to hurt me. Where's Rah?

Just as the teens arrived directly in front of him, Lenny felt the room quickly shrink. The walls seemed much closer than he'd remembered, and he felt the little air he had left being expelled out of the hallway. He continued to retreat until his back was up against the door and as he stood there, he threw his hands up in defense. Two of the assailants charged straight for Lenny grabbing him by both arms until he was immobilized. The third assailant delivered a forceful uppercut into his stomach, forcing the little breath he had out of him. He fell to his knees to catch his breath and looked up at his attackers. He was hopeful they would see his anguish and stop—he was wrong.

They landed each blow to his body and a few to his face until his chest fell to the ground. There was a ringing in his ear and his vision began to blur causing him to feel disoriented and helpless.

"Please…stop…help…please," he begged.

Lenny could taste blood in his mouth. Tears were running down his face and blinding him. All he could do was hold his hands and arms, now bleeding, in front of his face, desperately trying to stop their blows.

One of the inmates pulled his motionless body up from the ground, tearing his uniform in the process until he was barely on his feet. He held his face steady while another inmate walked up with a small razor blade.

"Smile bitch," he sneered slashing Lenny across his face.

The inmate holding him then delivered one final blow across his face until his body fell back to the ground and once again laid motionless in a pool of his blood.

He barely had consciousness as he watched one of the assailants turn his attention to the Irish inmate he'd arrived. With blurred vision, Lenny watched as they beat him until his body also laid motionless on the ground. He heard the inmate make a plea, which was also disregarded by the attackers.

"Please...stop."

From the ground, Lenny gave one final look up at his assailants and watched as one of their dirty boots came up from the cold concrete to connect with the side of his face causing him to go unconscious. All he could taste was blood as everything went dark.

CHAPTER 11:

BETWEEN HOLDING ON & LETTING GO

Lenny McNair

W hen Lenny finally woke up 36 hours later, he could barely open his eyes. He touched the bruise on his ribs and flinched in excruciating pain. His face felt numb and as he brought his trembling hands to his swollen lips, he cringed at the first touch. His face was covered in bruises, both eyes were puffy and slightly shut. Both cheeks had scrapes that were now beginning to scab over and he could feel the result of each body shot he took. His throat was dry and he felt another scab forming underneath his lip which came from the blade. He was in tremendous pain. He tried to talk but it burned his throat. He tried once more and this time the burning feeling returned in his throat and face even harsher than before.

What happened? He thought as he scanned the room to ensure he was safe. He first noticed the shackles tightly affixed to his right leg and connected to the bed frame. Next, he noticed a bible, like the one he'd seen in his grandmother's home, on the pedestal beside him. *I don't know if that will save me in here.* When he continued to peer around the room, he saw several beds with battered prisoners, some who screamed in agony while others just watched in terror at what awaited them outside of the infirmary. Like him, they were also handcuffed to their bed frames, and he could see their dread.

There were two nurses on duty and when he connected eyes with the older of the two, he watched as she shook her head and turned back towards her newspaper. Without looking up from her reading, she asserted, "the punching bag's awake," which accompanied the malicious grimace painted on her face. The slight stung Lenny's pride as he watched the second nurse turn her attention.

The second nurse, who was younger and seemed more enthusiastic at his awakening, walked over when she saw his eyes were open. She stood by his bedside, quickly scanned his chart, and smiled. Unlike the other nurse, she had a young face with naturally compassionate eyes, which he quickly took notice of. He could tell she hadn't been there as long as her senior, more bellicose colleague.

"Hello, Lenny. I'm one of the nurses on duty, Nurse Sharon. How are you feeling?"

Lenny stood silent and frightened. He avoided her gentle eyes, so she continued.

"Okay, Lenny. You don't have to tell me anything. I know how things work here."

She then walked away, and Lenny brought the covers over his eyes until he could no longer see the commotion he was hearing. He laid on his side in a fetal position and silently whimpered. He squeezed his eyes shut until his exhaustion carried him to sleep and he could no longer hear the commotion.

*****

By the next morning, after Lenny woke up, he saw both nurses were still there and stared over at the clock. He placed his hand on his ribs again to check if the damage had gotten any better but still flinched in pain. As he scanned, he could now feel the cloth patch on his uniform and realized he'd been given a prisoner ID number sometime during the night. He patted himself down further to ensure there were no fresh injuries he'd received overnight and when he was certain there were none, he *sighed* in relief. He'd been asleep for almost fifteen hours and assumed the two nurses were working a double shift.

I guess I'm stuck with them, and they gave me this number.

"Hi Lenny," Nurse Sharon remarked with compassion as she walked to his bedside.

"Hello." He was fearful and looked at her apologetically, on the verge of tears but knew he could not let one fall. He was still unsure where he was and what exactly happened but was sure he could not show weakness. "Where am I?"

"You're in the infirmary. The prison hospital. Do you know what happened to you?"

The details of the attack were still fuzzy, but Lenny could remember the immense fear that crippled his body as his attackers arrived at his location. A fear that quickly turned to desperation before he was knocked unconscious. After looking at the nurse, he turned his attention back to the ceiling which displayed his lack of cooperation. Lenny knew the code of silence and had no intention of making his time as PACC any longer or more difficult by being labeled a snitch. He didn't know her and didn't trust her.

"Lenny, I'm not going to ask you to do anything you don't want to do."

She then began to replace his bandages, causing Lenny to cringe in pain at her touch.

"I know it hurts. These injuries look bad, but we need to clean them to ensure there are no infections. I see here that you *just* got here yesterday and have already made a name for yourself. Let me tell you, in the short time that I've been here, it doesn't get any easier."

Lenny wanted to be tough in front of the nurse but laid worried about what came next. He remained quiet as she continued.

"You probably don't trust me and have no reason to, so you don't have to talk, just listen." She leaned in so Nurse Hadley couldn't hear them. "You and another inmate were found beaten, bloody, and unconscious in the hallway. I'm new here also so I'm still just learning exactly how things work. I'm not so sure what to expect but I need to find out what happened to protect myself. And you, of course. Perhaps there was a welcome party involved? Maybe some other inmates? Maybe some guards?"

Lenny was fearful but wanted to be tough. He'd only seen prison in movies and now he was stuck in one. He was frightened and his moral compass was telling him to hold firmly. Although he wasn't certain of many things, he knew that Rahzmel would have wanted him to keep quiet. He wanted to live up to his cousin's expectations.

I'm so scared. Does Rah know they beat me up? I don't know who I can trust here.

As he pondered, he began to find it more and more difficult to hold his tongue. His fresh terror and fear of the unknown made him want to tell her everything she needed to know as long as it protected him or got him released. His lips trembled as he looked at her, wishing she gave him one sign he could trust her, but she didn't. He felt conflicted and finally decided to keep quiet. "I don't know what happened," Lenny replied as he continued to hold his ribs.

Nurse Sharon saw he held firm to giving her any relevant information but also noticed how he reacted with a squirm when she mentioned the *guards*. She used this and continued.

"Lenny, from what I heard, the guards set you up to get beaten," she lied. "They did this to you, didn't they?"

Lenny looked up at her. *How does she know?*

"First I'm walking to my cell," he started. "Then I wake up here. I'm not sure what happened in between."

Lenny looked over at the door and saw a husky-looking guard peering into the infirmary through the specialized laminate material at the entrance. He tensed up and kept quiet.

"Okay, Lenny. Whatever you say." She knew she wasn't getting any more information out of the battered prisoner and finished wrapping his bandages. He didn't fully trust the nurse, and it was obvious to her.

I don't want to snitch but don't know who to trust here.

"Okay, Lenny, all set. You're going to be in here with me for a few days while you recover so get comfy. I want to monitor your recovery closely before sending you back. I'm here if you want to talk about *anything*."

He turned back to her and once again searched her eyes for safety. "Back where?"

Although he hadn't heard from Rahzmel, he was still hopeful that his cousin was working on his behalf.

"Back to your cell, Lenny."

I'm not a gangster. I shouldn't even be here. I can't believe I was so naïve to think this is what I wanted. Now I'm stuck in here alone and can't even protect myself. I'm so scared.

*****

By the time they'd reached the end of the week, Lenny was feeling slightly better and could now fully open his eyes. Thanks to the medicine and ice packs provided by the nurse, the swelling had gone down, and he could now walk on his own. The nurse had closely monitored his recovery and although he was grateful for her support, he still had no plans of revealing any details of what happened to him.

"Thank you, Nurse Sharon."

"You're welcome, Lenny. Good luck."

She's nice… unlike everyone else here.

At that same moment, an overweight guard with several arm tattoos arrived at the infirmary and proceeded to sign out Lenny for transfer back to his cell. When he noticed this, Lenny felt chills run up his spine. He felt a heavy ball in the back of his throat and knew he wouldn't be safe alone with this guard. His first two run-ins with the prison staff had resulted in harassment and a horrible assault, and he wasn't prepared to deal with another guard without an additional witness. He decided to take a shot in the dark and see if Nurse Sharon meant her words.

"Nurse Sharon?"

"Yes, sweetie?"

He leaned in to whisper. "Do you mind walking with me to my cell?"

The nurse turned her attention to look at the guard and then back to Lenny.

"Yes, Lenny. Let's go. I'll be right here with you to make sure you're okay. Don't worry."

When they arrived at the cell, He was relieved to see that he had the space to himself. He'd already lost the little trust he had in the guards and other inmates and could not bring himself to share a space with someone he didn't know.

Thank God.

"Thank you, Nurse Sharon. I appreciate you walking with me."

"You're welcome, Lenny. I'll see you around… hopefully not too soon or in the infirmary," she traded with a smile.

When he heard the cold cell door slam shut behind him, Lenny went straight for the one empty corner of the 8 by 8 ft prison cell. He slowly slid down to the floor, out of sight of the entrance, hugged his knees to his chest, and cried. He was already homesick and became nauseated at the fact that he felt trapped.

I can't do this. I can't do this. I can't do this.

He continued to cry until his legs went numb then moved to the bed, which was simply a thin mattress with a light blanket. As he lay there, the same question replayed in his mind.

Where's Rah?

Lenny remained in his bunk staring at the concrete ceiling for what felt like hours. Every time he looked over at the door, he hoped he'd see a familiar face staring back to return him to his freedom. Instead, all he saw was the burgundy metal door with chipped paint and grew anxious. He heard the commotion from other inmates outside in the hallway and became even more fearful. He was so terrified, that his body began to shake uncontrollably as tears fell from his eyes. The space of it suffocated him. He finally cried himself to sleep hours after he arrived at his cell.

*****

As he started to wake up, Lenny could hear someone calling for his attention from his cell door. When he wiped the sleep from his eyes and his sight cleared, he saw an unfamiliar face and disregarded the calls. He thought *I don't need to make any more enemies in here. I just want to be left alone.* He continued to lay without further acknowledging the calls.

"Kid, get over here," the older inmate remarked as he suspiciously looked around. "We have a mutual friend who sent me here to let you know he'd be reaching out soon."

Mutual friend? Lenny thought as he slowly turned his attention back towards the door. *He?*

"C'mon kid. I don't got much time before the guards come by for their rounds. Get the fuck over here."

Lenny saw the inmate's haste and slowly rose from his position to hobble over towards the cell entrance. The inmate looked much older than most of the others Lenny had seen up until that point and reminded him of his attackers.

"Listen…I don't want any problems. Just leave me alone."

"Listen, kid, I can tell you're new here and must not know how things work. This ain't the playground or middle school. You'll need friends in here if you're ever gonna make it through your bid."

"I don't want any friends in here," Lenny shot back softly. "I just want to be left alone. Please. Just leave me alone."

"I didn't say anything about what you *want*," the inmate roared back in condescension. "You'll *need* friends because we look out for each other. Protect each other from beatdowns. You know. Like the one you got the other day. Trust me…you'll need them in here. Anyway, I just came to see how you're doing. We can be *friends* if you want. You believe in God, right?"

Lenny could tell the inmate had been in the prison for some time by the way he stood with carefree confidence only long-time inmates exhibited. As he peered into the inmate's eyes, Lenny could see the same devilish smirk that Rahzmel wore many times before. The inmate continued.

"Don't gotta be afraid, man. We have a mutual friend who sent me to check on you. Heard there was some trouble and wanted me to see how you were doing. That's it. I'll ask again. Do you believe in God?"

Mutual friend? Lenny thought to himself. He looked at the inmate suspiciously but was desperate for any sign he could find that he had not been forgotten by his *friends* on the outside.

"Yes, I believe in God." *I don't know if he's talking about Rah or not. I should keep quiet.*

He looked suspicious and waited for the inmate to continue. The inmate said nothing and simply wore a crooked smile like one he'd seen his cousin make.

"Ummm… okay… Our mutual friend? What did they say? Am I getting out of here?"

"Listen… your guardian angel just sent me to check on you. Didn't say anything else besides that. You don't have to worry though. I'll take care of you.

I'll make sure nothing else happens to you because you're my *friend*. Right?" The inmate looked over and noticed the guard making his rounds. "I'll see you around."

"Wait!" Lenny interjected before the inmate fully disappeared from the small opening in the door. "Did my guardian angel say what I should do while I wait?"

"No…just keep your head down and wait. If you see any guards with the name Kellerman… do what that fuck says. He's a fat white man with a big beard. Don't get on his bad side. For your sake, you don't want his attention. Trust me. The best advice I can give you is to avoid him."

"Okay," Lenny replied in appreciation. "Thanks."

Sounds like that guard who checked me in.

He'd heard stories of the prison's nauseating food and disconsolate guards, but this was worse than he could have ever imagined. He proceeded back to his bunk where he was planning to continue silently crying.

I can't believe I'm stuck here for the next five years. How did this even happen? How could I be so fuckin' dumb?

When he finally sat up, Lenny noticed a bible, much larger than the one he saw in the infirmary or any he'd ever seen before, sitting on the pedestal beside his bunk. Because of its size, it closely resembled a dictionary and he used both hands to pick it up. *Why's this so heavy?*

When he opened it, he saw a small Motorola phone tucked inside a small cut-out located squarely in the center. He knew there was only one person who had enough power to sneak a burner phone into his cell before he even arrived.

Rahzmel? … It had to be him! He's the only one who can sneak the phone into a prison cell. Thank goodness! He must be trying to get me out. Lenny grew hopeful and found comfort in his assumptions. His original doubt had begun to dissipate, and he grew excited.

Lenny quickly turned on the phone and saw there were no saved phone numbers or recent calls. It resembled one of the burner phones Rahzmel kept around the Clubhouse and Lenny smiled.

I knew they didn't forget me. They wouldn't just leave me here!

CHAPTER 12:

THEY'LL TELL YOU YOU'RE THE VICTIM

Lenny McNair

Lenny sat for hours and impatiently watched the phone, hoping for a call but nothing came. He waited and waited and just when his excitement began to fade and his anxiety started to set in, the phone began to vibrate.

He rushed to the door to check for any guards and when was sure there was no one within eyesight, he crouched in the corner of the cell and answered the call in a hushed voice.

"Hello? Hello?... Who's there?"

"Lenny…"

"Rah?"

"Yeah, it's me. You alone?"

"Yeah, Rah. I found this phone and I'm in my cell, alone. Thank you. Thank you. Thank you. I knew you would help me."

"What did you get yourself into? You doing okay?" the kingpin offered in a manner Lenny hadn't heard in a while. Lenny could hear concern, which was now unusual for Rahzmel but brought joy to the jailed teen. "How'd they pick you up?"

"Rah, I swear I didn't do anything! I was just walking home, and they pulled up. I don't even know why. You know me, I didn't say anything."

"I hear you and I'm sorry, Lenny. I didn't know anything about it. From what I'm hearing, you got picked up by some overzealous detectives looking to make a name for themselves. I had no idea…"

"I believe you, Rah. They pulled up on me outta nowhere but I'm holding up okay. It didn't look like any of the cops I've ever seen you with."

"Lenny… now I'm hearing you were beaten up? That's crazy. You just got there. You okay?"

"Yeah, Rah. I'm good but I need to get outta here… please get me out of here, man. Some guards let a few inmates attack me and I was in the prison hospital for like a week. I *just* got out today. Please get me out."

"I'm going to do everything I can to get you out ASAP. Until then, I'll make sure you're protected in there. I won't let anyone else put hands on you again or they'll have to deal with me."

"Thanks, Rah. I know you will."

"Heard when the cops went to ask you questions, you ran? That true?"

"Yeah, Rah. I had a quarter pound of coke from the Irish and didn't know what to do. I'm not even sure why they dropped it off to me. When they gave me the money, they threw in the drugs too and I didn't know what to do so I took it and was planning to bring it to you, but the cops followed me and picked me up before I could. It was weird."

"All right, Lenny. Not the smartest move to run but we'll figure this out. Assuming you got my message at your arraignment?"

"Your message? You mean the woman?" Lenny questioned suspiciously.

111

"Yes. For obvious reasons, I couldn't be there but wanted you to know someone was there on my behalf. Called in a few favors to the police commissioner's office because I wanted to remind you that you're a member of this crew. This family and I are going to protect you. But for me to do that, I need you to keep your head down and keep quiet. You made a pledge to keep our dealings to yourself. You're still planning on keeping that pledge, right?"

"Yes, Rah. I don't plan on talking to nobody."

"Lenny... you've said this to me several times and somehow, we always end up in the same place. You saying more than you should and me having to scream at you for it. I really mean it this time. You need to keep a very low profile and speak to no one."

Lenny could hear the seriousness in Rahzmel's voice and could sense his older cousin's seemingly genuine concern. Lenny wasn't sure if this concern was for his protection or the wellness of Rahzmel's gang but knew he needed to reassure the kingpin that he had nothing to worry about.

"Don't worry, Rah – I know I've been a loudmouth in the past but that was around people I knew. I don't know anyone here and don't plan on saying anything about you or the others. I didn't even say anything when the judge told me my charges."

"Yeah... that's true... but from what I heard you said some shit about 'the people you're connected with,' which was dumb. It's stupid things like that I'm speaking about. You're not a gangster Lenny and don't gotta play one."

Lenny could hear Rahzmel's voice raising over the phone until he caught himself and continued.

"Listen, Lenny – if I had to guess, I'd say they may try to use the coke and money to find more information from you. That's what they do. They're going to tell you that you're helping a bigger cause but they just want to use you to get to others. They're going to tell you that you're a victim and that they can save you. They're going to try to get you to turn on the others who aren't in there with you. Those others being me, Croc, and the rest of the crew. Your *family*... "

There was a pause as both men waited for the other to speak. Rahzmel continued. "Lenny, just do your time till we can figure this out. Can you do that?"

"Yes... I can. You're my family, Rah, and I won't let you down."

"Okay good, man. Listen... you went out like a G," he traded with a laugh. "Runnin' and fightin' and shit. I'm sure I don't need to worry about anything with you and just wanted to share those reminders. You don't need to worry about a thing. I made some calls and you're now protected in there. Just keep to yourself and nobody else will bother you."

"Okay but they're saying I gotta be here for five years. You took care of that too, right?"

There was another silence on the phone.

"Right, Rah...?"

"Right, Lenny – I'm *taking* care of it, but it may take a little longer than I hoped," the kingpin offered.

"How much longer?"

"Not much longer. I just gotta figure some things out then we'll have you out soon. I won't let you down, Lenny. You're my family."

"Ummm... okay Rah. Can you tell grandmama I'm doing okay?"

"Sure, Lenny – I'll let her know."

There was another silence on the phone until Rahzmel continued.

"Lenny don't worry about anything. You're protected in there, and as long as you keep your head down and your mouth shut, we'll have you out in no time. No one else will fuck with you. I promise. You know you have a big mouth so keep quiet. We have a lot of friends there. There's only one number on this phone and it's to my direct line. Keep the phone close and I'll be checking in every now and then till we get you out. Okay?"

"Okay, Rah. Thank you."

Just at that moment, the phone went silent, and Lenny sat there hopeful.

If Rah said he's going to get me out, he'll get me out. This probably looks like the cell Frank Lucas was in. I'm going to be a legend when I get out.

Lenny stood proud and hopeful knowing his older cousin was out working on his behalf and assumed he didn't have long till he was out. Like Frank, he'd always known Rahzmel as a man of his word. He was usually the smartest person in every room he was in but also knew him to quickly be triggered. Although he did his best to keep it away from him, Lenny saw pieces of his violent side in the various business dealings he conducted that required it. Violence was always Rahzmel's last resort, but Lenny knew he was never that far removed from a decision that resulted in someone being hurt.

He attempted to go to sleep but was consumed by a terrifying sense of loneliness that brought him to tears. As each one fell through the night, Lenny finally drifted uncomfortably to sleep hours later in exhaustion.

*****

On his first day in the yard, Lenny approached with caution. The enclosure was filled with inmates of all sizes, shapes, and colors. The contrast between them was obvious and Lenny had no intentions of standing out. He simply wanted to keep his head down, mouth quiet, and blend in—just like Rahzmel had advised. He didn't know what to do or where to stand but knew he needed to go somewhere he could be inconspicuous. He slowly sauntered across the grass towards the crowded basketball court.

When he'd arrived, he found the first available space on an adjacent open wall so he could position his back against it to observe others—just like Rahzmel taught him. He'd already garnered too much attention from the guards and other inmates and wanted nothing more than to shrink himself to safe levels. As time went by, he continued to stand against the wall as others leered at him while passing by.

I don't know if I need to look like someone they can't mess with or someone who doesn't want any problems. He stood perplexed. *I think I'm just going to have to be someone who doesn't want any issues. I don't want to get beat up like that again.*

From his position, Lenny continued to watch his surroundings vigilantly and made general observations. He'd noticed the penitentiary was mostly filled with minorities, with ages he assumed ranged from fourteen to eighteen, and most of the guards were white. Although the yard felt "full," he could tell there were dozens of available cells spread throughout the cold facility begging for other lost teens to fill them.

115

In his initial observations, Lenny classified the inmates into two classes. There were the gang members, who were the obvious managers of the prison's underworld because of their existing relationships and control. Most had accepted their role in the crime which brought them to prison and flaunted it like a badge of honor. They made up more than sixty percent of the population and were always on the hunt for fresh talent to help grow their command. To them, their domination came from isolating their more senior members away from problems by manipulating new inmates into joining their ranks and performing low-level crimes. This allowed all gangsters to walk around with a cloud of presumed safety, which Lenny wanted but wasn't ready to pay for with his life the way he saw others had. To him, he'd already signed with the devil once and was still hopeful Rahzmel's word meant something. He wanted to be spared as the exception.

On the other end, there were inmates who still claimed their innocence and avoided the gangs. Lenny had dubbed them the "teamsters" because they usually walked around in clusters of five, but never more than ten, in order to ensure they were never caught alone and vulnerable. They mostly avoided violence—their safety came in their numbers and their ability to navigate around trouble when they sensed it. At the earliest sight of a crime being committed, these were usually the inmates who were the first to disappear. Lenny saw this group as his obvious cohort choice but still planned to remain independent as he still had hope in his cousin.

Although this day bore a wintery chill, most teens walked around the yard bare-chested with their uniform tops draped over their shoulders. A few of them had scars or gang tattoos and moved around in groups of three or more. He could tell this was not done in an effort to brave the cold. The new inmates had just arrived, and they were being recruited by the gangsters. It was hunting season.

*****

After two weeks had passed, he'd grown further concerned after he hadn't heard back from his cousin. Most of the other inmates he'd arrived with all seemed edgy and tense, and he began to worry for his own sanity. His initial excitement had now faded, and he grew very uneasy at his surroundings. He assumed Rahzmel was still dealing with the complexity of his situation and wanted to remain hopeful that he was not forgotten but struggled.

This is taking too long, he thought to himself often.

By day fifteen, Lenny still hadn't heard back and decided to use the burner phone to contact his cousin. He still wanted to trust his cousin's word and didn't want to put pressure on him but as each day passed since his arrival, so did his optimism.

"Yo, Rah. How's it going? Just checking in on how it's going. Haven't heard back from you. Any progress on getting me out?"

"Yeah, Lenny, good to hear from you. Sorry man, it's been *really* busy out here but we still working. Turns out, things were just a little more complicated than I thought. No big deal though. We still working to get you out soon."

"How soon Rah?"

"*Soon*, Lenny…" he growled in a tone intended to remind the teen who he was and what he's done. "Anybody else messing with you in there?"

"No. The guards and inmates don't bother me anymore and I keep to myself."

"Good, man. This means the protection I pay for is still working. Just keep doing what you're doing till you hear back from me. Ok?"

"Okay, Rah. Will do. Thank you. Do you think…"

The phone went silent before Lenny could get another word and he was once again left alone with just a fleeting optimism and blind appreciation for the work he assumed his cousin was performing on his behalf. He had more questions than answers but knew all he could do was hope. He locked his fingers together behind his head and stared at the ceiling in satisfaction.

I knew Rah would come through.

CHAPTER 13:

DON'T CRY FOR ME

Lenny McNair

After another week had gone by, Lenny still hadn't heard back and once again attempted to contact Rahzmel for an update. He was growing frustrated and impatient and wanted answers more than anything he'd ever wanted up until that point.

He first peered outside of the cell entrance to see if any guards were around, then crept back to the empty corner of his 8 by 8 foot prison cell. He slowly slid down to the floor, out of sight of the entrance, and dialed his cousin. On the first attempt, the phone went straight to an automated message from the phone carrier indicating the number was out of service.

No, this can't be right. Let me try again.

When he dialed the same preset number again, carefully looking to ensure each digit matched the number he received the original call from, it again went straight to the automated message, and he realized the phone number was now deactivated. *What the fuck's going on,* he thought to himself as he attempted a few more times—still getting the same result.

What are they doing out there? Can't be that fuckin' complicated. Where the hell's Rah?

Lenny grew angry at the thought of Rahzmel's absence. He still feared him and needed his protection but grew irritated with how his freedom was being handled.

Everything I did for those guys. Now they treat me like this? I can't believe it.

Lenny continued to debate his emotions. Although he wanted to be more upset, he still wanted to keep a shred of hope and reminded himself that Rahzmel moved like a ghost in order to ensure their shared safety.

Wait...He's cautious. Maybe he just swapped phones to make sure no one can track him. Yeah. That's got to be it. He wouldn't leave me like this.

This reminder softened his anger slightly, but he knew he needed to try something different.

I'm desperate and need to take a different approach. Let me try grandmama.

*****

As each day passed since his arrival at PACC, Lenny grew anxious when he hadn't heard from his grandmother. He'd regularly attempted to use the prison phone to contact her, but she did not pick up his calls. She was still very angry after his arrest and had refused to speak with him or come to the prison to visit. Her silence was piercing, and he was afraid she'd given up on him. He wanted to give her time but struggled and grew desperate when he began to feel like he could no longer depend on Rahzmel's connections. She'd already lost one grandson to the street life and Lenny knew she depended on him to be different. Her last piece of hope was that the sacrifices she'd made throughout her life were worth it.

Unfortunately, her hope was already hanging on by a string because of the disappointment suffered by the actions of Lenny's father and Rahzmel. Lenny knew he was supposed to be the one to break free but, instead, believed he was on the verge of finding himself in the same position his cousin and father were in—a failed investment.

After his unsuccessful attempt at contacting his cousin, Lenny used the burner phone and dialed his grandmother's house line.

I hope she's home. C'mon grandmama – please pick up.

As the phone rang, Lenny continued to peer around anxiously. His legs were wobbly, and he felt like he might throw up. He suppressed a shiver and felt his heart lurch as he waited. By the fifth ring, there was a response.

"Hello?" He started slow. "Hi grandmama, it's me. It's Lenny."

She remained quiet and Lenny could hear the screeching coming from outside of his cell. The commotion had garnered the attention of the guards who made their way to break it up. Although fresh terror reared up within him, he knew he only had a few minutes.

"Listen grandmama. Whatever they said I did, I didn't do," he lied. "I don't know whose drugs it belonged to or where they came from."

There was no response so Lenny continued.

"Grandmama. You there? Please talk to me. Please" His voice cracked.

"Lenny, what number are you calling me from?" She started slowly but gently. "It didn't say it was from the prison."

"I got a phone from someone in here so I could call you. You weren't picking up when I called you from the prison line, so I needed to try something else. I'm desperate."

"Lenny, are you okay? Are you alone?"

"Yes, grandmama. I'm alone." He didn't want to worry her with talks of his assault.

"Okay, Lenny. I'm sorry I haven't come by or picked up your calls. This has all been very hard for me, so I had to pray about it. You're a good boy. It's not supposed to be like this. I can't see my *only* grandson in a cage like an animal."

Only? He thought to himself before continuing. "I know, grandmama. It's all a big mistake."

There was another pause on the line and her tone softened further. Lenny could hear her sniffles and felt a heaviness in his throat. *She doesn't deserve this.*

"Lenny, I know you're scared. I'm scared too. I'll do all I can to help you get out. Do you have everything you need?"

"I think so. They feed us a few times a day and they have some snacks and stuff at the commissary. If you have a few extra dollars, do you think you can put something on my books so I can get snacks?"

"Okay, Lenny. I'll add money to your commissary. Is anyone bothering you in there?"

"No," he lied. "Everything's okay."

Lenny could hear the commotion outside of his room had settled and feared the guards were back on patrol.

"Listen, grandmama, I need to go now but I want to say I'm very sorry for all of this. I didn't mean to bring this trouble into your life. I pray you can forgive me and come to visit. I need you."

His voice was filled with regret and after his plea, there was another silence.

"Thank you, Lenny. I love you, baby. You'll see me soon. I'll come to visit. I promise."

"Okay, grandmama. Thank you."

Lenny left their call excited for her first visit and knew he had a long way to go to win back her favor but was ready to put in the work. The only other time he'd seen her this angry was when she found out Rahzmel was storing drugs in her home and kicked him out of their home and lives.

CHAPTER 14:

THEY CAN NEVER TAKE IT FROM YOU

Lenny McNair

On the day of his grandmother's first visit, Lenny entered the visitation room, hands still bound, and quickly scanned the room looking for familiar eyes. The space was brightly lit with dilapidated tables and low stools that spread across the large room. There were cameras affixed to the walls facing every direction of the room and guards on both sides of the bolted metal doors. Prisoners were allowed to sit in the open air across from loved ones but the guards closely monitored their dealings. There was no plexiglass partition to separate them, just a prison sentence and their shared regret.

His eyes quickly connected with his grandmother as he approached. The first thing he noticed was how much weight she'd lost and how the wrinkles in her timeworn face had emerged. He assumed it may have come as a result of him not seeing her for a few weeks and felt a sudden rush of guilt. At first sight, he felt his eyes begin to tear up but quickly wiped them away.

"Hi, grandmama."

"Hi, Lenny," she sighed and looked at him with a gentle reproach. She wanted to be mad, and Lenny could tell she was still figuring out if she was more disappointed or angry. She smiled wanly and looked at the healing scar below his lips. "Lenny, what happened?"

"It's okay, grandmama. Just tripped when I got here. Nothing to worry about. I'll be okay."

He'd mostly diverted his eyes away from hers but could see her eyes had tears welled up. He too was on the verge of breaking down but knew he could not allow his eyes to flood the way they were begging to. There were other inmates also in the visitation room and he could not let any of them see him like that.

"How are you, baby? Are you doing okay? You look like you lost some weight."

"I'm okay, grandmama. It's the food. It sucks but what can I do? You look like you lost some weight too. Everything okay?"

She began to sniffle as she continued to struggle to fight back her hurt. Because of his shame, he kept his eyes affixed to her body or the wall directly behind her. When he finally mustered up enough courage to look her in the eye, she broke down crying. It was not the sight of the tears that caught Lenny's attention so much as the sound.

"Yes – everything's okay," she offered with a hopeful smile as she wiped her eyes.

"Grandmama…I'm so sorry for everything. I swear to you this whole thing's big a mistake."

He watched as she sat with disappointment all over her face. She could tell he was lying, and he knew it.

"Lenny McNair, don't you lie to me. We come from a house of God, and he will protect us. Were those drugs yours?"

He'd never directly lied to his grandmother before and could not think of any worse situation to begin doing so. She'd always preached faith and he knew he

125

was long past asking for permission. His only option was to beg for her forgiveness and hope things could one day return to the way they were before he got involved with Rahzmel's operation. With deep regret painted all over his face, Lenny leaned in—eyes still avoiding hers.

"I'm sorry, grandmama. I lied to you. I did accept the drugs from some guys but wasn't going to sell them. I don't do that."

"Look at me, boy," she demanded. "Lenny McNair...look at me."

When his downcasted eyes looked up, he saw hope beaming from hers. "Lenny, what's done, is done – no time for us to worry about it now. We just need to focus on bringing you home."

His mouth fell in shock at her gentle response. He'd expected anger but was glad her faith had guided her this day. Lenny then looked around suspiciously then leaned in further to continue.

"You heard from Rah?"

"No, I haven't..."

Her face dropped as she replied in a manner that displayed her lack of surprise. "That boy's out destroying the world and don't care nothin' for us. You know I cut him off when he brought that poison into my home. What makes you think he'll call me now?"

"Wait, he didn't call you? You haven't heard from him at all?"

"No, why? Was I supposed to? Wait... did he get you mixed up in this nonsense?"

"No, grandmama. I did this by myself," he lied. "I just figured he would've called to check in on you since I was locked in here. You're still his grandmama too."

"Don't worry about him, Lenny. Worry about yourself. I've been speaking with some great lawyers who tell me that may be able to help you. Just stay patient."

"Thanks, grandmama. How are we going to pay for all this?"

"We'll find a way. God got us."

Lenny was not as optimistic as she was and continued. "Grandmama - you gotta call Rah. He owes us."

"No!" She roared back drawing attention to them. "I won't call that boy and we don't ask him for help. Ever. From what I'm hearing at the salon, he's got some new young kid running with him. Some black boy from the foster house in Canarsie, I think. He doesn't care about the family so let's stop talking about him. Listen, Lenny, the prosecutor's talking about a deal."

"What type of deal?"

"A deal they want to offer us to get you released."

"What do they want in return?"

"I don't know yet. I also think I *just* found a lawyer who I think can help us and we're supposed to speak again soon."

"Thanks, grandmama. Let's see if this lawyer can do anything for us."

"Keep your faith, baby."

"I'll try, Grandmama. It's hard in here with everything going on but I'll try. Every day, I wake up petrified or angry. Most of the other prisoners are angry kids and the guards don't care what happens to us. I'm afraid one day someone will..." He closed his eyes and braced for the end of a sentence which he knew would hurt him, but his words failed him. "I feel like everyone's against me and there's no peace."

She leaned in close to him and Lenny could feel her body heat radiating. "You can't expect peace to be given to you, especially in here. It's gotta be within you. If it's in you, they can never take it from you."

Just then, the guard entered the room and grabbed Lenny.

"I love you."

*****

After the conversation, Lenny made his way back to the prison yard to finish his recreation time. He'd developed a habit of smoking cigarettes, which had become his form of coping with his predicament, and lit one as he walked the grounds alone with his head on a swivel. He could see that most inmates had the same self-assured, casual air of menace. All heads were also on swivels due to the occasional altercation which Lenny learned could be triggered by something as small as a simple glance at the wrong person. For that reason, he mostly kept his head down and his feet moving.

Although he didn't consider himself a member of the Teamsters, he usually found himself walking in their shadow to deter others, especially the gangsters, who may have wanted to prey on him if he were alone. That, coupled with what he assumed was Rahzmel's protection, worked and occasionally, he found himself amongst various groups of Teamsters who were freestyle battling, slap boxing, or just sharing stories of their lives before prison. Lenny never partook in the activities but enjoyed the company.

*****

When he arrived at the concrete flattop on this day, Lenny stopped and watched as others went to war on the basketball court to entertain the observing guards. He'd grown up playing ball and still loved the game but couldn't bring himself to play at PACC. He recalled how most games when he was free would end with him and Oliver standing side by side in a shouting match with their opponents, or teammates, which was usually initiated because of his best friend's hot temper. He usually played the arbitrator in most situations and felt chills up his spine at how close he and Oliver had grown. He was proud of how close they'd become and missed their daily talks.

While watching the game, Lenny stood there inhaling the harsh cigarette smoke into his lungs to warm himself up on that cold December day. He was elated that he finally got to see his grandmother after so long but could not stop his mind from racing. Everything from her appearance to his cousin's lies replayed in his brain but there was one thought that held his attention hostage. A thought which echoed in his mind.

'Black kid from the foster program in Canarsie?' I hope that's not Oliver. I told him not to go back there and hope he listened. I hope that's not him...

CHAPTER 15:

STORIES FROM THE OUTSIDE

Lenny McNair

As he stood there, Lenny looked across the yard and saw the beefy-looking inmate whom he'd met on his first day in his cell. He appeared pensive and unapproachable but Lenny assumed there would be some familiarity and interrupted as he arrived at the inmate's location.

"Hey, man. What's up? Remember me? It's Lenny."

"Hey," the inmate replied shortly as his eyes darted everyone but into his own. "Nah I don't."

"Oh – it's me. Lenny. You mentioned we had a *mutual friend*."

"Nah I don't know you. What do you need?"

"Listen, man, have you heard from our mutual friend? Haven't been able to get in contact for a few weeks."

The inmate turned his attention to Lenny and looked at him suspiciously before turning back to the others. "Mutual friend? I don't know what you're talking about. I have no idea what you mean. You're probably looking for someone else. Do you need something or not? If not, you should keep it moving."

What's going on? Lenny thought. *I think this is the same guy.*

"Yo, man, you remember me. It's Lenny. I'm the guy you came to see at my cell a few weeks ago. You said our *mutual friend* sent you. Remember?"

Lenny was careful that his voice did not shift too much in key. He knew that word of his nervousness would make its way back to Rahzmel, and possibly the rest of the prison if he wasn't careful.

A dour expression overtook the inmate's smirk before he growled. "I don't know what you're talking about so you should probably get outta here, youngin'. I only talk to my *friends!*" the inmate roared back curling his upper lip in a sneer.

The inmate once again turned his attention from the other inmates into Lenny's eyes and stared at him with murderous intent, that pierced through him. Lenny felt the aggression blistering off him and took a step back to avoid the confrontation he knew was building. After his assault, he did not want any more unnecessary attention, especially the physical kind, and slowly backed away.

"Alright...Alright... Sorry, man. Must have you confused with someone else. My bad."

What the fuck's going on? Why did that guy act like he didn't know me? He just talked to me the other day.

While walking away, Lenny began to think about the series of events that led up to the current moment and began to connect the dots.

Wait... first I got beaten up when I first got here, then Rah sends this guy to my cell to check on me. Why's he acting like he doesn't know me?

Lenny knew the power his cousin had. He believed that if Rahzmel wanted him free, he'd be free and began to feel as if each of the instances that had occurred may not have been as random or isolated as he'd originally assumed. He began to feel like his time in prison was being manipulated.

I want to believe all of this is by mistake but I'm starting to think it's not a coincidence.

As Lenny made his way back to his cell, a cocktail of his fear, worry, paranoia, and blind loyalty began to suffocate his mind paralyzing him at every step. His forehead glistened and he felt a heavy ball in the back of his throat. He could feel his heart racing as he stuffed his shaking hands into his uniform pockets.

I don't know what to believe. Ughh…

He was also sick with terror and tormented because he wanted to stay true to his vow of omerta but was having a difficult time finding a reason to because of the constant unease he felt. His conflicted mind was in a complete state of panic and by the time he'd arrived back in the cell, his belly cramped up and his hands got sweaty. He no longer knew what to believe and began to fear the worst. He looked around his cell suspiciously.

Wait. Did someone do something in here? I don't think the bible is where I left it. Someone must have come in here. I don't feel safe.

Lenny's paranoia suddenly turned to sadness and then to frustration as he contemplated his circumstance. *I can't do this. I can't live like this anymore,* he thought. He knew the value of Rahzmel's protection in the prison but as time went on, he began to think about the value of the invisible coat of armor his cousin led him to believe was there. He believed the gift of protection was contaminated and of sin and violence but knew he could not risk losing it. Although he felt abandoned, as Rahzmel had threatened to do many times prior, he struggled at the thought of turning on his cousin.

I don't think I can turn on them. Wait, know I can't turn on them. They'd kill me.

The kingpin was a calculated risk to his business partners and colleagues, and an even more dangerous threat to his enemies, which Lenny had no interest in becoming. He wanted to remain in his good graces and knew the only way to do so from prison was to follow his command. He'd observed how his cousin's gratitude had always been mostly transactional and as time went on, Lenny began to feel as if the traction of his freedom was being written off. He was losing hope.

I know Rah got the resources to contact me if he wanted to, but he hasn't. I just need to lay low and keep my head down. When Rah's ready to get me out, he'll know where to find me. I'm in this by myself.

His grandmother's physical state was also still top of his mind, and he worried for her. She'd always been the strongest person in his life, but he could tell something was wrong.

I want to do more for her, but I'm stuck here.

*****

Two months had gone by since his grandmother's first visit and Lenny was convinced that he was stuck. He had officially been locked up for 90 days and stopped concerning himself with thoughts of Rahzmel or his freedom. He simply approached each day hoping for the best.

Fortunately for him, he still enjoyed the protection his cousin had arranged for, which allowed him to keep his head down and mind his business without attracting any unwanted attention.

Thankfully, after the incident in the yard with the beefy-looking inmate whom he'd met on his first day in his cell, nobody else bothered him and he could be just another young black teenager wearing a number on a prison uniform. Just another sheep in the herd.

Besides his occasional link-ups with other members of the Teamsters, Lenny mostly avoided other inmates when he could unless he needed something, which was usually only cigarettes or information. As a result of this lack of trust, he found himself regularly walking the yard alone to pass time. He saw how the gangs had controlled most of the prison and wanted no part of it. This life was no longer attractive to him, and he just wanted to do his time and go home.

He continued with this routine in the days that followed and just as he went to purchase more cigarettes from another prisoner whom he'd become friendly with, he finally learned who the "*young black boy from a foster program in Canarsie*" was that his grandmother had referenced during a previous visit.

The inmate, Latavius, had a plump face with dimples that appeared in the upper parts of both cheeks. He went by the nickname, "Peach" because of the close resemblance his face had to the fruit. His eyes were usually sleepy, but he had a calm face, which Lenny grew to appreciate. He was also considered a member of the Teamsters because he avoided the gangs, but didn't have a grandmother to add money to his commissary, the way Lenny did. To survive, he was in the business of retail, usually selling cigarettes, toilet paper, or bubble gum to his fellow inmates.

"Yeah, rumor has it there's some beef on the streets with some Jamaicans," Peach remarked. "The kingpin and his crew are trynna smooth things over but it's not looking good. Might be a war soon."

"What crew?" Lenny questioned.

He leaned in, flashing his crowded teeth. "You know, the crew the kingpin runs with. That big black guy, Croc, and that new young kid, Oliver."

Lenny's heart sank hearing his friend's name.

"You sure it's a young kid named Oliver? That's the young kid running with them? His name is Oliver?"

"Yeah, I'm sure that's what I heard," the inmate replied confidently. "From what I'm hearing, things are going well for them in the streets so they're trying to work it out with the Jamaicans to avoid further issues. Anyway, do you still want the normal pack of cigarettes? Anything else?"

They continued to walk the halls together and as they spoke, the two of them walked past a small group of inmates shooting dice in the corner. When they passed by, everyone in the group looked up before turning back to their game. As he passed, Lenny felt chills. He grew stiff and uncomfortable as he caught the gaze of one of the prisoners whom he remembered from his assault. He vaguely remembered his face but could not forget the scar that rested above his right eyelid, which he assumed was from a fight or attack. Although Lenny recognized him, he saw no light of recognition in his attacker's eyes and continued forward until he and Peach were out of sight.

"You all right?" Peach asked. "Looks like you saw a ghost or something."

"I'm good," he replied with a cracking voice as he attempted to change the subject. He hadn't spoken with Oliver since before his arrest and although he knew it was a long shot, he asked anyway.

"Hey man – think...Ummm...think you can get me a phone number?"

"Ummm... Of course!" Peach replied with confidence beaming. "Whose number do you want?"

"Can you get me that young kid's number? Oliver."

"The one who runs with the kingpin? Why do you want his number?"

"No reason, man. Seems like things are going well for him out there. Guess I just want some advice on things."

"Okay. Come check me tomorrow. I'll get that for you. Numbers going to cost the same price as a pack of cigs, okay?"

"Okay. That's fine. Thanks, Peach."

As he walked away, Lenny folded in his regret at the mistake he realized he made in taking his friend to the clubhouse. He thought about Oliver often during his first three months and now realized how deeply connected he still was to Rahzmel's operation, despite his desire to leave. He knew he could not leave Oliver to fall victim to Rahzmel's slick talk the same way he had and worried about how to help him. Now thanks to Peach, he had a way of contacting him to warn him.

*****

The next day, he did return to their spot and met with Peach. They exchanged their usual pleasantries before the merchant quickly pocketed the cash and issued Lenny a piece of paper with ten digits on it. To Peach, this seemed like just another transaction, and he disregarded the weight of the numbers but to Lenny, this was everything he'd been waiting for. To him, this was the first time he would be connecting with Oliver since his incarceration, and he was excited to hear his best friend's voice.

After their exchange, Lenny made his way back to his cell and when he was sure he was alone, he used the phone Rahzmel had given him to call the number. At first dial, the phone rang and rang, and just as Lenny was about to disconnect the call, he heard someone pick up.

"What up?" the voice stated haughtily.

Lenny was shocked to hear Rahzmel's voice on the line. He hadn't heard from his cousin in months and was surprised to hear him picking up a burner phone he was told was given to Oliver.

"Hello…Rah? It's me. Lenny"

Lenny heard his cousin huff in disappointment before Rahzmel responded. "Lenny? What the fuck are you doing calling this phone?"

"Rah, I haven't heard from you in months. What's going on?"

"Lenny, I'm sorry but there's nothing more I can do for you. I called all my contacts and tried my best," he said. "You just gotta do your time and when you're back out, come find me. I got nothin' else for you. I'm surprised they gave you five years, but you got it. You're tough, right?"

"But Rah. What about grandmama. What will-"

"Lenny!" He interrupted. "That's it! Grandmama was good before you and she'll be good after you. It's best you just keep her outta this and do your time. She's old and probably can't handle the fact that we're both failures now. This is the life you chose. Deal with it."

Almost instantly, the line disconnected, and Lenny was once again left abandoned and confused.

Why's Rah picking up Oliver's phone? Now I know where I stand with him. I'm on my own out here. I can't depend on him or Oliver anymore. He's got Oliver just like he got me, and I need to let him go. I need to do this myself.

*****

He continued to meet with Peach regularly to remain connected to life on the outside. He no longer depended on Rahzmel for anything and no longer assumed he was working on his behalf. He also realized Oliver was much more deeply involved with the gang than he'd originally assumed and recognized there was nothing left he could do for him. Rahzmel had shown him the extent of his power and Lenny now knew Oliver's fate was out of his hands.

Although Lenny knew he could not change things for Oliver at this point, he continued meeting with Peach for information on the activity of the outside world. When the merchant spoke, Lenny's attention never wavered. He usually nodded excitedly and smiled with gratitude each time Oliver's name was mentioned. He didn't know how he could help his friend but hearing his name meant he was still alive and well which brought Lenny enormous comfort.

Fortunately for Lenny, Peach didn't care for the minutia of why Lenny was interested in the stories, as long as he was a paying customer—which was thanks to his grandmother who regularly put money into his prison commissary.

If the money was ready to change hands as part of most transactions, Peach happily shared the chronicles he'd heard about from life outside of the prison. Chronicles that usually involved the Collective, violence in the streets, and the growing drug epidemic that plagued every borough of New York. Lenny made it a point to ensure he always received updates on Oliver without bringing attention to his intentions.

Although he tried his best not to, Lenny continued to think about Rahzmel as the stories from the outside came in. He thought about days when they were both much younger. Back when he lived in Harlem and Rahzmel was good-humored, and valued time with his family. When Lenny seemed like a priority for him, and his kindness came with no expectations. But then there was a point when things changed. Everything became different when their grandmother kicked him out for selling drugs and being a part of a gang. Rahzmel became darker, more aggressive, and glowered at Lenny any chance he got. It was almost as if he resented Lenny for being the one their grandmother chose. His appearance and personality aged, almost overnight, and he lost any remaining cheer that lived in his eyes.

Lenny then thought about the prosecutor's words at his arraignment and realized he had Rahzmel mostly right except for one point he had wrong.

'Kids who are convinced they will one day be the next boss.'

He could not think of any instance where Rahzmel had truly been *preparing* him to take over the empire.

His blind admiration for his cousin had come as a result of the man he used to be. A man worth loving but never truly loved anyone else the way he made it seem. He didn't see it then but saw it now and felt sympathy for his cousin.

Although he's strong in power, he's also weak in love. I can't believe I thought this was cool. I can't believe I wanted to be a gangster like him. I don't want any part of this anymore.

CHAPTER 16:

MISSING YOU MORE THAN NORMAL, TODAY

Lenny McNair

On this January morning, Lenny's grandmother had come for her usual Monday visit. She had developed a habit of visiting her grandson every Monday and Thursday, which Lenny grew to look forward to. Fortunately, she was retired so she had the time to pursue Lenny's case and regularly came with updates from their lawyer.

During her first visit, roughly a month prior to this day, Lenny noticed her appearance had changed but wasn't sure if it was a result of him seeing her less frequently or something else, so he didn't think much into it then. On this morning's visit, her face seemed pallid, and she had a sallow look. Lenny was excited to see her before she arrived and when she finally made it in, his excitement turned into concern. He could tell there was something else going on.

She hobbled into the visitation room with a limp Lenny had never seen before and wore a smile in her greeting that he believed hid something deeper. Her shoulders looked slumped, almost defeated, and she carried more bags under her eyes than he'd remembered. She showed symptoms of illness. She clearly was not herself.

"Hi, grandmama. Are you okay?"

"I'm okay, baby. I've got some news you want to hear," she remarked, quickly changing the subject. Her eyes didn't drift. She didn't blink. "I spoke with the new lawyer who's been speaking with the prosecutor about your case." She paused as she caught her breath, then continued. "They want to sit down and make a deal with you. That thing you said when you were arrested about who you're connected with interested them and they want to discuss a potential deal to get you released. Can you believe it!?!"

Lenny hadn't known the New York judicial system to be particularly kind to black and brown individuals and assumed there was a greater cost that his grandmother either wasn't aware of or wasn't communicating to him. He sat quietly so she continued.

"They want to meet this afternoon so I'm going to go get some breakfast and come back. I told them since you're a minor, I need to be present, which they already agreed to."

"Okay, grandmama but they didn't say exactly what they wanted in return? Seems strange that they want to help us *now*. I've been here for months already."

"No, not yet – they said we'll learn this afternoon. Don't worry, baby. I won't let anything happen to you."

"Okay – I love you, grandmama."

Before she got up and disappeared behind the door, Lenny made one final plea.

"Wait! Grandmama...please don't forget me. Please don't leave me here."

"Lenny...I'll be right back. I'll never leave you."

Just then he got up and disappeared behind the same egress he entered through roughly thirty minutes earlier. As he walked back to his cell, he thought deeply about his grandmother's appearance and grew further concerned.

There's something wrong with her...

Before going back to his cell, Lenny made his way to Peach's cell to pick up a fresh pack of cigarettes. When he arrived, Peach's half of the cell was cleaned out and it appeared as if he'd left. Peaches cellmate was also absent, and Lenny assumed he'd been transferred to another wing, so he sauntered back to his cell in disappointment.

Who will I get my cigarettes from now?

*****

Just as his grandmother had mentioned, they all reconvened in one of the prisons interview rooms later that afternoon. Lenny's grandmother arrived with their lawyer followed by the prosecutor who entered only moments after her. The prosecutor had his shoulders back as he entered the room which displayed the same confidence in him Lenny saw at the arraignment. It was obvious this was not his first go-round of this nature. He wore a tailored wool suit with no tie and had his hair combed back. He looked like he was in the business of giving deals, not negotiating them, and this was just another day in the office. It was obvious that he was not used to losing.

Moments later, the guard escorted Lenny into the room and sat him down beside his grandmother, then he began to walk out. The prosecutor saw this and stopped him.

"Ummm... excuse me, guard. Are these necessary?" he remarked pointing to the handcuffs still on Lenny's wrist.

The guard looked dumbfounded at the remark and instead of disputing the prosecutor's request, he approached the table to remove them. Lenny could see the guard's disregard and knew the prosecutor's safety was the least of his concerns.

"Thank you, sir," the prosecutor remarked looking back at Lenny's grandmother in order to ensure she saw his gesture.

The heavy door slammed shut and the prosecutor turned back toward the jailed teen. The first thing Lenny noticed was how the prosecutor had a sharp wardrobe that commanded respect. He knew he came for business.

"How ya doing, kid? They treating you okay in here?"

"I'm okay. Thank you for getting these handcuffs taken off. Are you here to get me out?" Lenny shot back avoiding the small talk he knew the prosecutor was looking for.

"We're going to try to work something out to get you released ASAP. I looked at your rap sheet and it doesn't make sense. You're not a bad kid, just in the wrong place at the wrong time. A stable home, loving guardian, *and* ambitious. Your grandmother tells me you'd like to get into business one day, is that true?"

"Yes," Lenny replied shortly while looking at his grandmother.

"That's great. I wanted to go into business also but decided to pursue law instead. You'll be great at it."

Lenny sat silent as he waited for the prosecutor to get to the point.

"Alright, kid, let's cut to the chase. I know you're currently doing time that you shouldn't be doing. Sadly, you had a quarter kilo of coke on you, and we can't just ignore that. Turns out, that was a part of a large shipment that had just come into the country. The DEA is breathing down our necks on this one and we need to find out who and where it came from. We also need to know who's running it on the streets."

"I told you...it wasn't mine!"

"I know, kid. I know. Sadly, you were left with the bag so you're here to carry the weight of it BUT I want to help you."

Lenny turned his attention back to his grandmother then their lawyer, who was staring intently but made no sounds. The prosecutor continued.

"We want to bring down the entire operation to prevent any other kids like yourself from falling down this path."

Like Oliver, Lenny thought to himself. *I shouldn't be here, and neither should he...*

"We need your help.... Now I know there's a code of no snitching on the streets and fortunately, we're not asking you to do anything besides confirm details we *already* have to connect some dots."

"Connect dots? What exactly do you want me to do?" Lenny questioned suspiciously looking at his lawyer.

"We'll show you some individuals we know are involved and need you to confirm roles. That's it. We already have a credible witness who's already given us plenty but we need this. We need this from you."

"That's it? What do I get in return?"

"Your freedom. If your information pans out, we'll release you."

His grandmother interjected.

"Sir, you don't live where we live. Word gets out that Lenny cooperated with the DEA...we're as good as dead. We can't go back to Brooklyn."

"I understand that ma'am and I discussed that with my boss also. We're prepared to enroll the two of you in our witness protection program. We'd relocate you, provide a monthly stipend for five years, and grant immunity to any crimes you're currently convicted for. It's a clean rap sheet, kid. A chance to start over."

Lenny looked at his grandmother who looked excited at the deal. He wanted to share her enthusiasm but instead, wore nothing but doubt at what was being asked of him. He then turned back to the prosecutor.

"Can I think about it?"

"Yes, of course. I know it would be a big decision for you so we can give you time to think it over." Sensing his advantage, the prosecutor pressed on. "Sadly, the DEA is aggressively looking for answers so I cannot give you *too* long. Maybe a few days at most. I'll keep them at bay for you."

"Okay." Lenny turned to his grandmother and saw her smile. "I'll see you on Thursday, grandmama?"

"Yeah, baby. I'll be here. I'll call you when I get home. I love you."

"I love you too."

Lenny's confidence grew as he walked. He was happy to see someone was still working on getting him out.

After Lenny left the visitation room and started to head back towards his cell, he heard others talking and one scoff, "that fuckin' big mouth!" Hearing the anger in the inmate's voice stopped Lenny dead in his tracks. He leaned back against the wall and slowly peeked around the hallway to see who was talking. He recognized the inmate with the scar right away and just seeing him made Lenny's stomach turn with nervousness. From Lenny's vantage point, he couldn't make out the face of the other inmate.

"The kingpin said we had one chance to rough him up and we'd be paid for life," said the inmate with a scar. "He still hasn't sent any money and it looks like we may be stuck with him for a while."

"So dumb, I guess the boss doesn't know the system as good as he thought."

"Right! No way carrying that much coke would only be one year, even with no priors."

"Guess it did more than just scare him. Let's just call the big guy tomorrow to see if we can get paid otherwise, we need to do something to the loudmouth."

Lenny was frozen in shock.

Was this all a setup?

He realized he had Rahzmel completely wrong and turned tail and darted back to his cell.

By the time he'd arrived, Lenny was shaking in fear. He could barely see straight, and his throat became dry. His breathing has picked up rapidly to the point of hyperventilation and he was sweating profusely. He stumbled to the sink to splash water across his face and as he did so, his knees began to weaken so he quickly rushed over to his bed.

Rah did this? Did Rah set me up? He could barely believe it as his mind raced. *He wouldn't have. Right?*

He sat forward on the cold mattress, elbows on his knees and hands clasped together. He stared at the cell entrance blankly hoping for someone to show up with a sign. He needed a sign that would reveal what he should do next or who he really could truly depend on.

Although he didn't fully trust anyone in prison, he still had a fleeting hope that Rahzmel was not behind the blueprint of his arrest or assault. He'd already given up so much and didn't want to feel scared anymore. He just wanted it to be over.

Maybe I should just let them kill me. That way, I won't feel this way anymore. I don't want to be scared.

As these thoughts began to encroach upon his mind, he pictured his grandmother. He imagined leaving her in a world with just Rahzmel and was taken back. She was his reason to keep fighting and he needed to stay optimistic.

How can I leave her like this? I can't...

CHAPTER 17:

SAVE YOURSELF

Lenny McNair

L enny used the days which followed to think about the inmate's admission and also thought more about the prosecutor's deal. He knew his grandmother was growing older, and possibly ailing from something she was not telling him, but struggled to find ways to help her. He was tired of wasting time in prison and grappled with a decision.

She needs me and I'm stuck in here.

He also worried for Oliver. He continued hearing perilous stories of Rahzmel's operation and assumed Oliver's involvement grew as the operation continued to flourish. His friend was walking down the same path he himself followed and there was nothing he could do to stop him.

Someone needs to tell him to make better decisions than I did. Besides grandmama, Rah was my only other connection but now I don't know what to believe about him.

He was conflicted and spent days debating which direction to take. By the time the weekend had arrived, Lenny felt closer to a decision but far from one he was comfortable sticking behind. He became further vexed with the complexity of his situation.

If I cooperate with the DEA, I'll be labeled a snitch and can never go home to Brooklyn. Grandmama and I will have to move and look over our shoulders every day. I don't think I can put her through that. Also…I don't know if I can believe those inmates. They are liars and thieves after all, and Rah's my cousin. My blood and he's already done so much to protect me. I really can't believe everything I hear.

He continued to debate. *But if I don't cooperate, they'll keep me in here for the full five years and I don't know if I can do it. I'm not a gangster like those guys and I don't know if I ever will be. I don't think I'll ever live up to Rahzmel's expectations and don't deserve to be here with these people.*

As he continued to wonder, Lenny's thoughts once again began to focus on the prosecutor's words about him being 'left to carry the bag of others.'

I wonder if any of those guys would take this deal. I wonder if they ever snitched to save themselves.

Lenny's mind raced through the night until he heard the bell ringing that Saturday morning. The sun's rays shot through the small window in his cell momentarily blinding him and causing disorientation. He felt fatigued, conflicted, and anxious, and knew he needed some help to calm his nerves. Because of the treatment from the guards and the assault that came at the hands of other inmates, also seemingly arranged by the guards, he no longer felt safe in his cell and isolated himself in the cold corner.

In his first three months of incarceration, there was only one place where he'd felt he could breathe and think. A place he didn't need to worry about other inmates attacking him and could just be. Even though he was still planning to keep his head on a swivel, he knew he needed to be back at the infirmary. He needed some help.

*****

As he'd seen others do, Lenny submitted a request to visit the infirmary for a follow-up to his original visit. He hadn't been to the infirmary since his assault and followed the step of completing request documents, submitting them, and waiting for his application to find its way to the top of the list for approval or rejection.

On his documents, he indicated he was suffering from non-life-threatening issues related to his poorly healed wounds and requested a follow-up visit to see Nurse Sharon. He then left it with the guards and prayed for the best.

Almost 48 hours later, a guard came to bang on his cell door loudly with his baton.

"Inmate. Stand up."

"Where are we going?" Lenny questioned in suspicion.

"Shut up and lock your hands together."

This doesn't seem right...

Lenny apprehensively did as instructed and hobbled through the hallways until he stood in front of the infirmary entrance.

Thank God, he thought. *I don't know what to believe anymore.*

He connected eyes with Nurse Sharon, who quickly shot up from her desk to approach Lenny with concern.

"Lenny? Is everything okay?"

Lenny stood demurely when she said this. "Hi, Nurse Sharon. I'm okay. Haven't been back since my first day. Just wanted a follow-up appointment."

She knew he was lying. "Uh-huh. Sure. They all say, *'nothing's going on,'* then wind up beaten and bloody. I see the scar under your lip healed well."

"Yes."

"Lenny, why are you back?"

"I'm having a hard time sleeping. I got a lot on my mind. Wondering if there's any medication or something you can give me?"

"Medication for sleep issues? No, we don't carry that."

He stood silent, with disappointment painted all over his face. She continued.

"Lenny. Talk to me. What's *really* going on?"

He paused and searched for allyship in her eyes. He knew he couldn't voice his suspicions too outwardly because he feared what would happen if Rah got the slightest inclination of his betrayal. "I don't think I can or should talk about it. I should just leave."

"Why, Lenny?" she remarked placing her hand to stop him from exiting the room. He stared back into her face, again looking for any sign he could find that he could fully trust her. There was a pause before she continued. "You're in trouble, aren't you?"

"What?"

At that moment, the door opened, and Nurse Hadley entered so they both became silent until she walked into the back office and closed the door behind her.

"Look, Lenny… the first time you were here, I was very concerned about you. What was done to you. When I walked you to your cell, you looked so scared, and I knew I shouldn't have left you alone there but there was nothing I could do for you. I thought about you often until recently. There's something I heard about a week or two ago that really concerned me. I really don't want to get involved with the prison politics or gossip but after that beatdown you received; I was very worried."

"Worried about what?"

"Lenny… what are you involved in?"

"Nothing…I swear!"

She stood disappointed. "Lenny, I'd like to believe you, but I can't. I won't dig too deeply but I'm concerned. For your safety and mine. Another inmate was in here about two weeks ago and had received a similar assault as you. He could barely open his eyes or speak for days before we saw signs of recovery. When he woke up, I sat with him, and he confided in me. He was petrified…just like you. He was reluctant at first but finally told me his beatdown was arranged by some big-time gangster on the outside who had some connections in here. His face had been slashed like yours and your injuries looked alike, so you came to my mind. All I'm saying is be careful, Lenny. Please."

What's going on? he thought to himself. "Nobody bothers me, and I want to keep it that way. I don't want any problems. I just want to go."

"Okay, Lenny. Nobody bothered Latavius also until they came for him."

Lenny turned his attention towards her, and his eyes widened in disbelief. "Wait…the inmate…his name was Latavius? Are you sure? Does he have big cheeks and always look tired? Does he go by a nickname? Peach? Are you sure?"

"You know him? she remarked with obvious concern.

"Ummm… yes. I've seen him around."

He still had a startled look on his face, which Nurse Sharon took notice of before she continued. "If you say so. Just know, this is very serious, and I know you have no reason to trust me but you should know you can. I've only been here for a short time but I'm seeing how things work. I'm realizing this isn't what I signed up for."

*****

Lenny laid in the infirmary bed for the rest of the afternoon and by the time the sun had gone down, he knew his time in this safe space was ending. Nurse Hadley was wrapping up her shift and came out with a smirk as she turned off the office lights and entered the main room.

"Time to leave," she badgered in satisfaction.

"What? Where's Nurse Sharon?"

"Do you think she'll let you stay here? I don't know what the fuck you think is going on here but whatever it is...you're wrong." She dropped her bag on the desk and stared at Lenny square in his eyes. He'd avoided hers so she continued. "I told you whatever game you're playing better not mess up my money and now you're playing with my patience. I'm officially off the clock; they don't pay me to deal with this shit."

"I just want to talk to Nurse Sharon. Please," Lenny begged.

"She's gone and you need to be too." Nurse Hadley grabbed his arm forcibly in an attempt to drag him out, but Lenny snatched it back. The irate nurse looked shocked at his response and then made a second attempt, but Lenny shot to his feet.

"Guard!" she yelled. "Guard, help!"

A husky guard who stood outside of the room rushed into the room and restrained Lenny. Nurse Sharon also arrived back in the room at the same time and rushed in to stand between Lenny and Nurse Hadley.

"What's going on here?" She questioned looking the guard in the eyes as a lioness would when protecting her cubs from predators. "Why are you restraining my patient?"

"He tried to attack me," Nurse Hadley scowled back.

"No, I didn't! She grabbed my arm, and I took it back. That's it."

"Liar!"

Nurse Sharon looked at Lenny then to Nurse Hadley then back to the guard. She noticed Lenny was wide-eyed and trembling. "Sir, this patient is under my care and I'm monitoring him overnight. He's here because we're evaluating him and he's in no condition to leave."

She handed the guard Lenny's signed documentation, which he disregarded as he attempted another objection. "But…" Before he could continue, she interrupted.

"But nothing! Do you want me to tell the warden you forced me to send an inmate back to the general population against the doctors' orders? Don't think so."

Both the guard and Nurse Hadley looked at Nurse Sharon with cynicism, and Nurse Hadley shook her head as she walked out of the room. "Whatever, he's your problem," she remarked grabbing her coat and purse.

The guard also shook his head and followed her out of the room.

"Thank you, Nurse Sharon. I'm sorry for the trouble."

"I'll be paying for that later. Lenny are you okay? Seems everywhere you go, trouble seems to follow. Why are you still here?"

There was a silence. *She helped me. Maybe I can trust her...*

"I lied to you before Nurse Sharon. I'm worried. I'm afraid what happened to Latavius will happen to me again. I don't know if I can take much more of this."

Lenny paused for a moment, looked at the door to make sure Nurse Hadley was gone then continued. "I do know Latavius. People call him Peach. He's my only friend here. We hang out every now and then, and now I know why I haven't seen him in a while. Is he okay?"

"Lenny - This is very serious. Latavius died."

Lenny's eyes widened, his mouth dropped, and he stood speechless.

"Dead?"

"Yes, Lenny. He died and you probably would have too if you hadn't made it here in time. Like you, he had multiple fractured ribs and a razor blade slash across the face, but the internal bleeding was too much. He died on his way to the hospital."

I don't know what to believe. If Rah set Peach up and set me up too, then I'll never fully be protected in here. I loved him but I can't trust or depend on him anymore. I can't stay here...

Lenny paused as he looked at her, once again searching for safety in her eyes and when he finally felt like he found it, he continued slowly.

"I need to get out of here. I can't do this anymore. I shouldn't be here. My grandmama wants me to do something that may get me out, but I'm scared. I don't know if I can."

Nurse Sharon stood in shock, but not surprise, and leaned in to comfort him.

"Lenny, I can't tell you what to do or decide for you but if what we talked about today is true, you're not safe in here. Your friend died and it sounds like you both may be a part of something much larger than even you understand. I don't believe you're safe in here." She placed one hand on his shoulder to comfort him then made one final plea.

"If they're giving you a chance to get out, please take it. I can't protect you in here, but they can out there. Please get out of this hell and go live your life. You're so young and have so much ahead of you."

CHAPTER 18:

THE SOUND OF YOUR TEARS

Lenny McNair

When he arrived back at his cell, Lenny had finally made up his mind about what to do. Nurse Sharon's warning was the confirmation he needed and he was ready to finally leave this nightmare he'd endured for the past few months.

I'm done with Rah. He's the only one who could have gotten Peach beaten like that. Just like me...He had to have orchestrated this whole thing. He set me up from the beginning and just abandoned me. Now I know why I haven't heard from him in two months. I'm done protecting him...I'm done...

By the time Monday came around, Lenny was ready to once again sit down with his lawyer, his grandmother, and the prosecutor. When they gathered that afternoon, the jailed teen stared straight into the prosecutors' eyes and got right to business.

"I'm ready to cooperate, sir. I'm ready to give you what you need to get me out of here."

Lenny's lawyer interjected as he reviewed the paperwork.

"I also looked at the documents, Lenny. Things look good. Everything that was promised is outlined here and we're close to getting you out."

"Okay. Thank you."

The prosecutor reached in his briefcase and placed a document on the desk, which Lenny's grandmother quickly reviewed and then signed before passing it over to her grandson who signed it without hesitation. He turned and looked at his grandmother, wishing he could embrace her with a tight hug. The guard standing outside the door saw his look and smacked the metal door with his baton when he saw Lenny slowly motioning towards her.

"Great, Mr. McNair! What comes next is we'll return on Thursday to take your statement. Once we have the statement in place, we'll sit down with the DEA and determine if the information is enough. If so, we'll present you with documentation to get you released and added to the witness protection program. You made the right decision here. We're on the right track."

We better be. Lenny thought. *I need to get out to take care of my grandmama and I'm not safe in here...*

*****

By the time Thursday came around, Lenny was once again escorted to the same interview room to meet with the prosecutor, his lawyer, and his grandmother. He was now more confident because he was excited that others were working on his release and felt a fleeting feeling of cockiness that he was close to his release.

When he entered the room, he noticed there were two additional individuals Lenny hadn't seen before standing in their ill-fitted suits, each leaning against the wall in two separate corners. Unlike the prosecutor or Lenny's lawyer, these individuals had pensive looks on their faces which Lenny took notice of as he entered.

The next thing he noticed was a video camera facing the one available seat, which he could tell was for him.

"What's going on? I wasn't told I would be on camera" Lenny inquired.

"Lenny, these gentlemen are from the DEA. I told you we are working on a deal together and they're here to ensure your information pans out. They need the footage to share with their higher-ups. Don't worry, it's all a part of the process."

Lenny looked at his lawyer, who shook his head in agreement at the arrangement. He then looked at his grandmother who had a forced smile of encouragement. He was still uncertain if he felt comfortable with the arrangement but knew he needed to follow their directives to move forward. He slowly motioned towards the chair.

"Please have a seat, Mr. McNair. The DEA will now take over this interview. Good luck."

As Lenny sat, one of the DEA agents walked over to the camera and turned it on to record. He sat quietly beside it and stared straight into Lenny's eyes until the teen turned his attention down towards the table.

"Mr. McNair, my name is Anabel Green with the Drug Enforcement Administration. I will be asking you a series of questions that I'm looking for you to answer clearly and honestly. Do you understand what we're here for?"

Lenny looked over at his grandmother and then back to Anabel Green.

"Yes, Mr. Green."

"Okay great. Good start. Let's start slow. What's your name and how old are you?"

"My name is Lenny McNair and I'm sixteen years old."

"Okay good – and Mr. McNair, what are you currently incarcerated for?"

"I'm in prison because I was arrested with some drugs and money on me."

"What drugs were on you at the time of your arrest?"

"Cocaine."

"Do you know where the cocaine came from?"

"No, I don't"

"We have reason to believe the cocaine you were arrested with was a part of a larger shipment that was recently smuggled into the United States of America. According to our information, the cocaine operates as one of the primary sources of revenue for a New York-based crime syndicate. Do you know anything about this?"

"No, I don't," Lenny replied suspiciously trying to protect what dignity he had left.

"Have you ever heard of the drug *creedo*?"

"No, I haven't."

"Dealers take packs, just like the one you were arrested with, and cut it with baby formula and other ingredients. It doubles, sometimes triples, their profit but comes at a cost. The drug becomes even more dangerous when it's cut improperly. The result of that is creedo, which unfortunately is very addictive and continues to pollute the streets of New York. People are dying every day from it."

"Okay, I don't know anything about that."

"Yes, I'm sure," replied Anabel Green in an arrogant tone. "Mr. McNair, have you ever heard of an organization called 'The Collective?'"

Lenny's face dropped. Until then, he didn't know the full extent of the information the DEA had access to. He assumed they had nothing significant and were looking for him to substantiate the little bit of information they did have—which he was prepared to do. He knew exactly what the Collective was and began to worry. Although he was angry at Rahzmel, his fear quickly overtook and crippled him. He knew his cousin's reach extended deep and was once again afraid to cross him. He needed to answer cautiously.

"Yes, I've heard of it," Lenny replied looking back at his grandmother for her shock or disappointment. "They tell stories about them back in Brooklyn. Just a few gangs or something like that. I don't know much else," he lied.

"Do you know any of these gangs within the Collective?"

"No, I don't." He paused and again looked at his grandmother. "Well, maybe I've heard of a few of the local street gangs being a part of it. Like the Jamaicans and the Hispanics."

"Thank you, Mr. McNair. Do you know any of these individuals?" Mr. Green slid over five headshots of Latino men, whom Lenny did not recognize. He exhaled in relief.

"No, I've never seen them before. Who are they?"

"That's what we're trying to figure out, Mr. McNair."

Lenny could see Anabel Green's impatience growing. *I wonder if I've given them enough. I hope so,* he thought.

"Mr. McNair, do you know Liam Walsh? He's a top member of the New York chapter of an Irish gang," Mr. Green slid a mugshot in front of Lenny and observed as Lenny's face changed in recognition. He could tell Lenny knew or knew of this individual and leaned back in his chair in gratification. "Mr. McNair?"

"Sorry, Mr. Green - I think I recognize the face."

"Is he a member of the Collective?"

"I think so."

"Sorry, let me rephrase that, Mr. McNair. We *know* he's a member of the Collective. Is he the one who gave you the drugs?"

Lenny was stunned at how much he knew and became tripped up in his responses. He wanted to cooperate, but his mind was growing fuzzy as he realized they may have known more than they let on. *How do they know? How much does he know? Shit.*

"No...uh...yes...wait...no, he wasn't the one who gave me the drugs. I never met that guy before. Just heard about him and seen him around the neighborhood."

"You've seen him around? That's strange. Liam Walsh usually hangs around Park Slope, which is far from where you live. Where have you seen him around?"

"I'm not sure. Probably in passing."

"In passing? Just in passing like you go to the same barbershop?" he replied sarcastically. "Yeah, right."

"No..."

Anabel Green shook his head in disappointment. He reached over to stop the recording, clicked his tongue, and let out a large exhale. He looked at his partner, who looked down at his wristwatch, then back to the prosecutor, who looked nervous. Mr. Green then turned back to Lenny.

"Mr. McNair, I believe you're here cooperating with us to get released, correct? You're here of your own free will?"

"Yes."

"So why does it feel like I'm here convincing you to give us information? If you don't want to work with us, we'll leave and let you get back to your cell to finish your *full* five-year sentence. We don't need to be here," he emphasized to make his point.

"I'm sorry. I'm telling you everything I know but tripping up on some of the details. I'm nervous and my mind's fuzzy. Can I please have a glass of water?"

Mr. Green could see the perspiration that had formed across Lenny's face and reached into his breast pocket for a napkin. Lenny's breathing had rapidly increased, and they all watched as his grandmother began patting his back. She interjected.

"How much more do you need from him? He's doing the best he can. Lenny's a good boy. We're a God-fearing family and Lenny is a good boy! If Lenny was involved in any of this, it's because someone made him."

"I know, ma'am. I do. Trust me. We just need to make sure this is airtight. I get the sense that there are gaps in Lenny's story and my higher won't accept that. Trust me when I say I'm here to help you both."

"No, I'm telling you all I know!" Lenny interjected.

"But you're not telling us *everything*. Stop wasting my time if you want to go home."

Although Lenny was used to using his slick-talking ways to avoid challenging situations, he knew this was one he could not get himself out of. He couldn't risk his freedom.

Mr. Green isn't playing, and I don't think I can avoid this. I just need to confirm what I know about Liam and the Irish.

"Maybe I know a little more. I'm sorry, I didn't know how much detail you wanted and got confused. I'm a little nervous. Sorry."

"Lenny, we want everything," Mr. Green demanded impatiently. "This is the second time I'm asking so let's begin again and don't leave out a thing. Tell me everything…"

"Okay."

Anabel Green turned the recording back on and turned back to Lenny.

"Who is Liam Walsh and how do you know him?"

"You can protect me and my grandma, right?"

"Yes, Mr. McNair. We can and will protect you if your information helps us."

"Okay – Liam Walsh is one of the top guys with the Irish crew. I knew him because… I got the drugs from him."

"Okay good. Now we're getting somewhere. Why did he give you the drugs?"

"Because I was supposed to sell it for him?" Lenny replied as he looked over at his grandmother in shame. She did not look shocked at his revelation and simply wore a look of disappointment, which Lenny knew he would eventually have to answer for at a later time.

"You work for the Irish?" Mr. Green questioned apprehensively.

"No. Not really work for them. I just got to know them because they supplied me with drugs, and I sold them. It wasn't a regular thing. Just a few times."

"You're telling me that you cut this kilo of coke and sold it?"

"Yes - but not all the time. Just once or twice because I needed money. I also didn't add all that other stuff to it as you said."

165

At that moment, Mr. Green pulled out another picture from his folder and slid it across the table. To Lenny's surprise, it was a picture of him standing beside Liam's car on the same day the Irishman delivered the drugs to Lenny's school.

"Thank you for your honesty, Mr. McNair. We *know* Liam gave you the drugs and were looking for you to confirm it. About a month ago, someone anonymously tipped us off and claimed drugs were being sold at the school. They left this and didn't leave any other information, so we had nothing until we connected with the prosecutor who pointed us here. Mr. McNair, are you telling us Liam Walsh supplied you with the quarter kilo of cocaine you were arrested with, and it wasn't the first time?"

"Yes, that's correct."

Mr. Green smiled and then turned off the camera. He looked at his partner who hadn't moved from his spot in the corner during the entire interview.

"This enough?"

His partner shook his head and Mr. Green turned back to Lenny.

"Thank you, Mr. McNair. This is great. We just need to shoot this interview up the chain and can begin to process your release. Shouldn't take more than a few days."

Just then, Mr. Green and his partner shook hands with the others in the room, including Lenny, then departed.

"When do I get out?" Lenny questioned while looking at the prosecutor?"

"Just give them a few days. They'll let us know if the information you shared is enough."

"It has to be. That's everything I know, and it has to be enough."

"I'm sure it is, Lenny. Just be patient and keep your head down. We'll hear back from them soon. Okay?"

"Okay. Thank you."

The guard then came into the room to grab Lenny and before walking out, the jailed teen gave one final look back at his grandmother and saw her wiping her eyes. He'd assumed these were tears of disappointment for his revelation and looked at her with shame painted on his face. He expected anger, even yearned for it, because it meant she still held feelings for him and carried hope. It meant she did not abandon him as so many others had up until that point including his father, his mother, and even Rahzmel. She was the one person he could not afford to lose.

Although he hoped for it, Lenny didn't see anger in her look. Behind the tears was a smile. One he hadn't seen in months but remembered as his beacon that as long as they were together, things would always work out.

"I'll be home soon, grandmama. I'm coming home. I love you."

"Take care of yourself, my love. I love you. Take care."

As he ambled back to his cell, Lenny could not stop thinking about the last sight of her. A smile that gave him comfort and tears so silent that he imagined a beautiful score playing the soundtrack to his freedom.

CHAPTER 19:

I CANNOT GO BACK

Lenny McNair

Over the following days, Lenny impatiently waited for any update that would bring him closer to his release. He knew each day that passed since he made that recording was a greater risk of someone finding out what he'd done, especially Rahzmel, and regularly inquired about the status of his release. As each day passed, his anxiety grew.

Lenny found it difficult to shut his eyes at night. Before bed, he would check to ensure his cell door was securely bolted and none of his items had been tampered with. He wrapped stacks of papers around his chest to prevent himself from being stabbed and placed extra toilet paper in his shoes to make them snug. He wanted to be ready in case he needed to break out sprinting at a moment's notice. He also replaced toothbrushes daily to ensure he wasn't poisoned and constantly relocated his bible to different hiding spots around his cell.

On this day, he went to grab the bible to relocate it, as he'd done every day since he first met with the DEA. When he looked inside, he noticed the phone was gone.

Where the hell is it? Someone was in here. Rah must know... I need to get out NOW!

He slid down to the floor, out of sight of the entrance, hugged his knees to his chest, and cried. He sat and waited hours for the guard to announce it was time for him to make a call. When he did so, Lenny rushed over to the bank of payphones and called his grandmother.

"Grandmama, are there any updates? When am I getting out?"

"Sorry baby, I don't have any other updates. We're still waiting." She couldn't sense his level of desperation and continued as if this were just another conversation. "Listen, Lenny, it's nothing for you to worry about but I've been a little sick. I'm getting treatment for the minor ailment."

"Grandmama, what?"

"I didn't want to worry you, baby, but now that you're almost out I wanted you to know. By the time you get home, I should be 100% again. Nothing to concern yourself with. Trust me."

"You sure, grandmama?"

"Yes! I'm doing okay. It's just my old age and a poor diet finally catching up to me. Let's not waste time thinking about this…Let's just focus on getting you out, okay?"

"Okay, grandmama."

I couldn't even tell her how afraid I am. I don't want to trouble her with this.

*****

One week after recording the video interview with the DEA, Lenny sat in bed contemplating his grandmother's illness and struggled knowing there was little he could do to support her. He couldn't shake the feelings he was experiencing, which teetered between helplessness, paranoia, and anger, and thought about her often. He felt helpless at the fact that there was nothing he could do to take her pain away and angry at himself because he was wasting time in prison. As he normally did, he contacted his grandma this morning to check in.

"Hi, grandmama. How you feeling?"

"I'm okay. Just a slight cough here and there. The doctors say I'm doing much better, but this is old age for you. I'm getting better thanks to God."

"I'm worried about you. I wish I could be there with you."

"But you are here with me. You're still praying for me, right?"

"Yes, I am. I think about you all the time."

"Then you're right here with me, baby. Just have faith that I'll be okay."

There was a pause on the phone.

"I'm going to get outta here soon. I need to help you."

"Thank you, baby. I know you will."

"Grandmama, how are you paying these doctors? Is your social security enough?"

"Yes, it's been enough. Don't you worry about that, Lenny."

"Grandmama, you know I know when you're lying."

"Don't worry, Lenny! We'll be okay! When you get out of there, we'll be together again and that will be all the healing I need. Have you heard anything back from the DEA?"

"No, grandmama. Have you?"

"Nothing yet. Just keep your head down in there. You'll be out soon, and we will be together again."

"I will. Thank you, grandmama. I love you and will see you soon… hopefully."

I'm wasting so much time just sitting here. I need to do more. I need to get out of here. Rahzmel's a piece of shit and I can't depend on him for anything anymore. I know she can't afford her treatments and he isn't even helping her. He probably doesn't even care. He's not the person I thought he was. The DEA needs to get me outta here.

Just as he sat fuming over his cousin, one of the prison guards used his baton to knock loudly on Lenny's cell to get his attention.

"Inmate, your lawyer's here."

Lenny's eyebrows raised and his voice became feeble. He'd *just* spoken with his grandmother, and she hadn't mentioned a visit during their conversation. He didn't know what to believe but knew there was something else going on.

"Did he say what he wants?" Lenny questioned suspiciously.

The guard looked at him disbelievingly. "Do I look like your fuckin' secretary? You want to see them or not?"

Lenny paused for a second. The last *time the guards called me like this, I was beaten up. I shouldn't go. Wait... but what if my lawyer really is here and I don't go. What if he has an update on my release? Why didn't my grandmother know? I hate these games. I hate being terrified all the time. I need to get out. I can't do this anymore. I guess I need to go...*

"Yeah, I'm coming."

When he arrived in the room, he noticed it wasn't his lawyer, as he'd originally been told. Both his grandmother and the prosecutor were also absent and as he slowly made his way into the room, Lenny saw it was just him and Anabel Green the room. He exhaled a sigh of relief when he walked in and saw he wasn't being set up.

What's going on? Where's everyone else?

"Mr. McNair. Great to see you again. How are you faring?"

"I'm good. Where's my grandmother and my lawyer?" Lenny questioned.

"I'll be honest, I didn't let them know I was coming because I came straight over from my office. We hit a little bit of a snafu with the case, and I rushed over here to speak with you before this entire thing blows up in all our faces. I couldn't wait to convene everyone else together."

"What do you mean?"

Mr. Green paused then exhaled loudly.

"Lenny, our credible witness who was supposed to make this case airtight has gone missing."

Lenny grew worried. He took notice of the fact that Mr. Green had addressed him by his last name for most of their interactions but now used only his first name during this bombshell revelation. He knew something was wrong and wore the surprise on his face. Anabel Green took notice of this and continued when he saw he had Lenny's undivided attention.

"Truth be told, we would have come back to you sooner, but things have been a bit crazy, and…well… things have changed a bit for you also."

"For me? How?"

"Yes, we needed that witness to help us make arrests and prosecutions, but now that they're gone, we have nothing… nothing but your tape which, as it stands, isn't enough."

"Okay, so what does this mean?" Lenny remarked in a hopeful tone. "What does this mean for me?"

"Means we can't let you out of prison just yet."

Lenny's heart sank. *I can't believe this. A week ago, I was in the process of being released and now I'm stuck here. I knew I couldn't trust these cops, the prosecutor, or the DEA. Now they have a tape of me snitching. I can't fuckin' believe this.*

Mr. Green looked at Lenny and could see him panicking.

"Mr. McNair, I'm not going to lie to you. I want to say there's nothing to be concerned about but that just wouldn't be true. You're facing your full five-year sentence…"

Five years. Oh my God. No…this can't be happening. No, no, no…This can't be happening…

"…*and* from what I'm hearing, your grandmother is sick. That's why I didn't want to force her to come all the way down here today for this convo. She isn't doing well Lenny…"

How does he know about my grandmama? I just found out. How could he know?

"…Mr. McNair, I think I can help you but will need you to help me. We can no longer just have you confirm details. I need you to take it one step further."

"What do you mean?"

"We need to stop this operation by any means possible and need to ask you more questions."

"Okay, I need you to get me out of here. What details do you need me to confirm? Details like before?"

"Yes…somewhat similar."

He's lying about something. I can tell but I don't care. I need to get out of here. I can't do five years. Not after they have a tape of me snitching. I need to get out of here. I need to be there for her.

"Okay but if I give you anything else, I need to get released *today*. I cannot wait any more days for things to fuck up again. No more of your guarantees or promises. If I give you anything else, you need to get me out TODAY! I can't go back there."

Lenny covered his eyes to hide the tears that he knew had formed during his petition. He was conflicted, fatigued, and knew if he'd left that room with anything but his freedom, he would be serving his full sentence. He lost faith and wanted to be released immediately.

"Okay, Mr. McNair. I can see this is important to you," he traded. Mr. Green had an opportunist look in his eyes and brought upon a smile that seemed forced but reassuring. "I really want to help you get released but you need to give us *everything* we need. This can't be me pulling information out of you. Not sure if you've heard but there's some war brewing back in Brooklyn. There were just four murders last night. I don't want to send you back to that. Do you want to go back to that life?"

"No, please just get me released and my grandma and me into witness protection. I'll give you whatever you need."

"Great, so we have a deal? We'll let you out and you will give us *everything* we need?

Lenny paused. "Yes – just get me out of here. I cannot go back to my cell. I need to get out today. Please."

"Okay, perfect – wait here. I'm going to get your lawyer in here and make this happen ASAP. I don't know if we can get your grandmother in time so can we get this done without her? That would most likely delay this a few more days. Do you agree to another interview? Also, can you confirm you're waiving rights to have your guardian present, correct?"

"Okay."

"Sorry, Lenny. We need a yes or no."

"Yes"

"Great! Wait here."

CHAPTER 20:

WHAT HAVE I DONE?

Lenny McNair

Lenny sat in the interview room for an hour until his lawyer and the prosecutor showed up. Upon their arrival, they both looked shocked to see Lenny sitting in the room without his grandmother. When they peered over to Mr. Green they watched as he nodded his head to indicate he had everything under control. Before his lawyer could get a word in, Mr. Green flipped on the camera, which was positioned directly in front of Lenny, and began.

"Same routine as before, okay?"

"Yes – okay."

"For the record, today is Thursday, February 28, 1985, and we will be conducting our second witness validation interview with Mr. Lenny McNair." He turned to Lenny and his face grew serious. "Mr. McNair, my name is Anabel Green with the Drug Enforcement Administration. Before we begin, can you confirm that you're sixteen years old and have given us the okay to proceed without your guardian?"

"Yes, as long as it gets me out today," Lenny replied apprehensively.

"Okay and are you here under duress?"

"No."

"Is the testimony you will give us the truth."

"Yes, it is. I will give you everything I know in exchange for my freedom today."

"Great, Mr. McNair – in a previous interview, which was conducted exactly one week ago, you mentioned Liam Walsh provided you with the cocaine you were arrested with. Do you know where he got it?"

"No, I don't."

"Perhaps it was from a colleague. Do you know any of his colleagues, Mr. McNair?"

"There's one guy I know named Sean, but I don't know much about him or anyone else in their gang. I think he's the driver."

"Thank you, Mr. McNair. Sean was the one driving on the day you were given the drugs, correct?"

"Yes - that's correct."

"So, it's safe to assume Liam and Sean were both aware of the drugs and money you were given on that day, correct?"

"Yes, that's correct. They both knew."

"And you believe Liam Walsh, Sean, and their Brooklyn crew are also members of the crime syndicate known as the Collective, correct?"

"Yes, I believe they are."

"Okay." There was a pause as Mr. Green reached into his briefcase for a folder. He turned back to Lenny and slid pictures in front of him as he proceeded with his next set of questions. As he recited each name, he slid a corresponding picture in front of the jailed teen.

"Lenny – Who are these individuals? Rodrigo Topaz, street name 'Rio.' Chequan Chen, street name 'Chino.' Cornell Crooks, street name 'Croc.'"

As Mr. Green pulled the last picture from his folder, Lenny's face grew warm. The original anger that he had towards his cousin had subsided and grew nervous.

Oh no...

His heart erupted with fear as Anabel Green slid the last picture in front of him.

"And last but not least, Rahzmel Davis, street name 'Kingpin.'"

Fear gripped Lenny as he stared at pictures of his cousin and his gang. He could not bring himself to produce any words and just stared at the pictures in disbelief. Up until that point, Lenny assumed the DEA had their sights set on the Irish gang and was shocked to learn their investigation was much farther than he'd originally assumed.

I can't believe it…

"We know he's the boss. He's the head of all of this, isn't he?"

Lenny's head dropped and his silence was deafening.

"Mr. McNair, remember why you're here. Your grandmother is probably sitting at some hospital waiting to *die* while you're rotting away in here! We need information from you to get you released *today* and we'll call your grandmother and tell her to pack. We have a location for your witness protection selected and just need your information."

Lenny continued to stare at the photo in silence until Mr. Green continued.

"Mr. McNair? Mr. McNair?!?"

"That's my cousin… Rahzmel. That's my cousin and the others are his friends. He doesn't have a nickname. Some people call him the kingpin, but he doesn't call himself that. That's Rahzmel and his friends."

"You mean his gang, right?"

With tears welled up in his own eyes and a ball in his throat, Lenny looked Mr. Green square in the eyes and said, "Yes. That's the gang."

"Are they members of the Collective?"

"Yes."

"What role do they play in the structure of the greater collective?"

"Rahzmel is the boss. The others are a part of his gang, and their gang runs the Collective. The other crews, like the Irish and Hispanics, each have their own leaders but, in some way, shape, or form, they all report to Rahzmel…"

Lenny paused and wiped his eyes.

"…Look, Mr. Green, these are very dangerous people. We're not safe in here or out there. I need to get out today. Please."

"I know, Mr. McNair. That's why we're here. To bring this organization down and get your released today. You won't have to worry about them after you leave this room."

Mr. Green saw the hope growing in Lenny's fearful face and continued.

"Thank you, Mr. McNair. With your testimony on Liam Walsh and Rahzmel Davis, we're going after all of them with RICO. You don't need to worry. Thank you for your cooperation. We've actually already contacted your grandmother and she's waiting outside with both of your bags packed. She's already signed the paperwork and with your forthcoming signature on the paperwork, we can send you both off today."

"Wait, my grandmama's here? Why didn't you let her in?"

"No time, Mr. McNair. She arrived as we were speaking and frankly, we needed your complete attention. We got everything we needed and once you leave this room today, we never need to see each other again. Your recording will be used to help continue to build our case which I'm hoping we have ready this year. Until then, you lay low and take care of yourself."

Lenny looked at Mr. Green nervously and made one final request.

"Listen, man, there's going to be a lot of talk about what happened to me and how I got out. We need to make something up because no one's going to believe I had a super lawyer who got me out after serving only three months in jail for that many drugs. That just doesn't happen for people like me." He peered over at his lawyer who observed the slight and continued. "We need to make something up like I got into a fight and died or something."

"Do you think that would help?"

"Yes, it would. It has to. Please… Please have the warden make up a rumor that I got into a fight with the guards for running my mouth and they accidentally killed me while trying to restrain me in a chokehold. Ask him to corroborate the story with the prison doctor, Nurse Sharon. This way no one will come looking for me. Please."

"No one like Rahzmel?" Mr. Green questioned.

"No one like *no one*. Can we make that happen or not?"

"Yes, we can, Mr. McNair. If it helps you, we will make it happen."

"Thank you."

At that moment, Lenny's grandmother rushed into the room with tears running down her cheeks. She hugged Lenny tightly and he could finally feel how frail she'd become over his three-month incarceration. He hadn't hugged her like this since the morning of his arrest and did not want to let go.

"Grandmama, I'm free?"

"Yes, baby. You're free. You're free," she remarked wiping the tears from under his eyes. "We can't go back to Brooklyn but today we start our new lives. I've always said we'll get out of Brooklyn one day. This will be our reset."

"Where are we going?"

"I don't know but we'll find out when we get there."

Lenny's breath grew short in anticipation as he looked over at Anabel Green, who slid paperwork across the table for him to sign. His hands were sure as ever while Lenny's quivered. His grandmother saw this and placed hers over his—helping him sign on the dotted line before signing in her section. Mr. Green reached out his hand to complete the transaction before the ink could dry and Lenny knew there was no turning back.

"Congratulations, Mr. McNair. You're officially a free man. No one will stop you as you exit today."

"Where are you taking us?" He remarked, his voice was tremulous with suppressed excitement.

"I'm not sure. For your protection, I cannot know. You're in the hands of the U.S. Marshals now who are waiting outside to take you *home*. I will work through their office if we need more information but as it stands, we do not plan to trouble you any longer. Best of luck to you both."

At that moment, Lenny looked at his grandmother and once again embraced her. As they stood there, all the tears he'd held back through his lengthy interview, and three-month sentence, suddenly erupted and he could not stop. The anger he once held towards Rahzmel had completely melted away and all that was left was his pity. Though Lenny had shown nothing but admiration for his cousin, the one thing he wanted in return was more than Rahzmel was willing to pay—his acceptance for who Lenny was: his blood.

Despite all the feelings he was experiencing, Lenny also could not stop thinking about what he'd paid for his freedom. He knew he'd been paying with the lives of others, which included Oliver since he first joined his cousin's organization, and he was ready to cash out.

He made his way toward the exit and as the large metal door closed behind him for the final time, he exhaled a sigh of relief. He just stood there, with a look of incredulity that the day he'd dreamed about for months had finally come. He couldn't stop staring at his grandmother's smile, which brought him comfort but could not shake the one question his mind could not seem to escape.

What have I done?

PART III
I USED TO DREAM ABOUT YOU

CHAPTER 21:

PRISONERS

Oliver Burke   **Present Day**

"The day I got out, I cried so hard I thought I was going to die," Lenny remarked as he wiped his tears while staring at the lake. Oliver could tell it was hard for him to tell his story and patted his back gently as Lenny continued. "They put my grandmama and I into a car with the darkest tints and drove for what felt like was forever. I didn't even know where we were going until we got there but when we did, '**Welcome to Orchard Hills**' was the first sign I saw and it read in the brightest blue letters I have ever seen. I'd never even heard of it before that day which made me feel a little good because that meant it was in the middle of nowhere. I just wanted to disappear. It was a small town with barely any black people but the U.S. Marshal's said we'd be safe there. He said we needed to stay close to New York in case I needed to come back."

"Come back? Why would you have needed to come back?" Oliver questioned.

"I don't know. The Marshals only said the DEA requested me to be close in case they needed additional information. They confirmed the story of my death worked and my file was erased but they still needed me apparently. I could barely believe it when they told me. I was finally *free* from prison, *free* from Rahzmel, and *free* from a life I barely had control over but was still in far deeper than I knew."

Oliver stared intently as he dropped his head. *I know the feeling,* he thought before Lenny continued.

"They said the case could take about a year and advised me to keep my head down. They coached my grandmama and me on stories of our new life and gave us new identification. Charlie Waters was the name they gave me. Do I even look like a Charlie?"

Oliver smirked. "No, you look like a Lenox."

Lenny smiled and shook his head in remembrance. "Those were the days, man, but I don't go by that stupid nickname anymore. That was a different life that I gave up a long time ago." Lenny paused. "I ran, man. I've been running my whole life. I thought that if I ran fast enough, my failures wouldn't catch up to me, but I was wrong. They were there every time I thought I was breaking the cycle. Every single time, the sadness was there."

"What do you mean?" Oliver questioned with earnestness. "It sounds like you left prison and moved into something better. When did you run?"

"I mean in general, man. I struggled to fit into Orchard Hills. It was hard actually but thankfully, it was my grandmama and me. As long as we were together, that's what mattered. She always said we'd get out of Brooklyn and when we finally did, it didn't matter where we went. We were together and it was a chance to start over." Lenny paused as he shook his head and smiled. "It was supposed to be something good for us but every day, I walked around with this heaviness in my heart. Although I was gone from Rah, I still felt like I needed to look over my shoulder every day, and did. I couldn't get comfortable there…"

"Lenny, that was a lot for anyone to deal with," Oliver traded. "Being taken from your home, sent to jail, and put into witness protection. I can't imagine what that was like for you. What I still don't understand is how you got arrested and sentenced just like that."

"What do you mean?" Lenny questioned. "They caught me with the drugs."

"Well, my friend Juan works with me at the youth center. He's also a public defender and I'm sure he could have gotten that case thrown out."

"Yeah, my public defender didn't seem to know much. It was almost like he was there just for show."

"But also the judge and prosecutor," Oliver began. "I don't understand why the judge would go straight to a decision and sentencing. I don't know much about the legal system but that seems wrong."

"Oliver...after I was in jail, I stopped asking questions. I saw how little power I had over my life and accepted whatever came. I lost my faith."

Oliver stared and nodded in understanding. "I had no faith either. Not until my mom showed me what miracles looked like."

"Well, I wasn't so lucky. Imagine convincing yourself that things will get better at each phase of life but as you move from one point to the next, something is taken for something else to be given. You know like they say, 'to whom much is given, much is taken.' Well, if you can imagine that, you can imagine what it was like for me."

Lenny coughed up the phlegm from his throat to clear it then spit it into the lake. He wiped the layer of sweat that formed on his forehead because of the oppressive heat before continuing. "Shortly after we arrived in Orchard Hills, I finally learned what my grandmama was dealing with. It was Chron's disease," he paused as his voice broke. When he tried to keep talking, his voice continued to crack. He squeezed the inner corners of his eyes with his thumb and forefinger and held this for seconds before finding his voice. "That was what I sensed the whole time, but she finally told me when I got out. She said she didn't want to bother me with it. Do you know what it is?"

Oliver wore empathy in his glare and nodded with a doleful simper. "No."

"Just picture someone slowly deteriorating from the inside until they can't manage the pain any longer. That's what it is. As time passed, she could no longer hold in food and the pain seemed unbearable. I cried myself to sleep every night as I sat next to her bed and watched her slowly go. After a few years of watching her suffer, she passed away in her sleep. I was right there, man."

"I'm sorry, Lenny. I know how much you loved her. You used to talk about her all the time," Oliver offered with deep sympathy in his voice. As Lenny spoke about his grandmother, Oliver thought back to his own mother and the similarities in their stories. Like himself, Lenny was also a prisoner who lost the most important person to him because of one man's greed and wrath. *This sounds like Ma.*

"Thanks, man. She was there for me, and I was just glad to be there when she needed me at the end. It was as if her time clock had sped up and life started pulling layers off her."

Lenny paused and cleared his throat again. Oliver could tell he was trying to hide his sniffles and whatever ailment he was dealing with.

"Like a week after she passed, I got a call from the Marshal's office. They said there was an urgent message and asked me to come into the office. When I arrived, Mr. Anabel Green was there with the Marshals and before he could even say a word, I broke down sobbing. I couldn't take any more bad news and knew he didn't drive all that way *just* to check on me. I was so scared I didn't even want to hear it. I'd just lost my grandmama and thought, '*what else can they take from me?*' Honestly, I didn't have anything else to give… or so I thought. I was wrong. They gave me something back that day."

By now, the sun was at its highest point in the day and the humidity forced Oliver to roll his sleeves up to stay cool. As he did so, he watched as Lenny's eyes traded between his cigarette and the lake and could tell his friend was dependent on this harmful vice. Lenny continued.

"Mr. Green told me Rahzmel and his whole gang died in a house fire in some uppity neighborhood in Brooklyn. He said there were no survivors in a way that lacked any remorse, and I could tell he was happy to close the case. My cousin should have rotted in jail before dying for the things he'd done, and we all knew it.

"I can't describe the feeling I had that day, but it was somewhere between sadness, anger, and joy. I was angry because Rahzmel didn't suffer the way the rest of us had to under his care, but I guess that's the way things go sometimes. My grandmama was gone and there was no one left to pay for it. If we'd just stayed in Brooklyn, she wouldn't have had the stress and probably would have never gotten Crohn's. Rahzmel did that to us and I could never forgive him. Suddenly,

I felt joy and relief. He was *finally* out of our lives but the cost of that came in exchange for my grandmama's life. This was too high. The last feeling I had was sadness. I was still sad because of my grandmama's passing but I also thought you died in the fire. I asked about you, but the Marshals said Rah's name, Chino, Rio, and a few others but none of the casualties were named Oliver."

There was a silence and Oliver watched as Lenny exhaled all the burden he'd carried on his shoulders for nearly three decades. Lenny wore a downcast look on his face and Oliver could tell he'd been waiting to get all of this off his chest for a while. He watched as a gentle solace formed in his demure expression as he spoke about his grandmother. As he did so, Oliver sensed Lenny was glad she wasn't around to witness his own perils and failing health. It would truly have crippled her.

Lenny saw he still had Oliver's attention and continued. "But he was a coward, my cousin. Although he was smart, he didn't have the heart to do the things he asked others to do. He was a weak man. He let everyone die in a house fire because he was looking for money. At last, that's the story I heard."

Oliver watched as Lenny spoke about his cousin and his feelings during his recount of his life. He could sense Lenny did not know the second part of his story. The part of his story that changed everything for him. *He must not know… He probably doesn't know what happened that night. What happened to me…*

"Yeah, I heard that story also," Oliver admitted. "But I don't think it was about money. Rahzmel was smart but greedy. He thought he was untouchable and wanted power and control. All he did was take from everyone else until there was nothing left." Oliver could feel his voice rising and watched as Lenny turned his attention to him.

"That's right. He was like Dr. Jekyll and Mr. Hyde," Lenny paused. "He used to have good days that made you want to be around him all the time. But his bad days were really dark. He used to say we were at war. Not a military war, like the Afghanistan war. He used to say our war was silent. We were all fighting for money, power, and respect. The ones who got all three were the quiet ones. The dangerous ones no one ever saw coming. He would say I was too loud and could never win a war that way. What he didn't tell us was what the war would cost."

"We were kids," Oliver responded with anger. "His war cost us everything."

"I know. I know… Back when I was still living in Harlem and he used to come to visit, he used to say he was looking forward to getting out of the life, but he felt '*stuck.*' He was running with a gang for so long that I don't think he ever saw any other life. Deep down, I think he envied me because I did have a choice when it got bad in Harlem. I got to move to Brooklyn with our grandmama and I think he hated it. I feel like he blamed me for having the things he couldn't when he was my age. A family, true friends, and a choice."

"It sounds that way. After Rahzmel and your grandmother died, what happened to you? Where you in Orchard Hills this whole time?"

"Yeah, I was. I was stuck. After Rah and the others died, the government was pretty much done with me. The money continued for a bit but then it cut off and I was left to figure things out. The band-aid was ripped off and I found myself back in the hamster wheel that life forced me into. I thought I could escape it the harder I ran but it didn't work. It felt like the harder I thought I was running towards something better, the further I got from something good. My grandma was gone, I thought you were gone and now I was left in this place I didn't fit into. I was all on my own. That's what I mean I ran."

Lenny continued to divert his eyes and Oliver could see he was embarrassed. Lenny had reddened, watery eyes and Oliver sympathized with him. He placed a hand on Lenny's shoulder to express his support for what he was dealing with. Lenny looked over and smiled before continuing.

"Well after some time, the money from the government ran out and I ended up doing some odd jobs for money. That's when I ended up meeting a local girl named Keisha. She didn't have much either, which is why I think we connected, but she still helped me. I told her about my grandmother, and she looked out for me. Gave me clothes, fed me, and helped me adjust to Orchard Hills. Guess she felt bad.

"Well, Keisha lived with her mom, but she was never home, so I used to go over there a lot. As you can imagine, both Keisha and I were young, horny, and alone so we did what anyone in our position would have done. We did it for years but unfortunately, she got pregnant real young. We tried to hide it for a while but after she started showing, her mom surprisingly let me come stay with them. She knew I had nothing, and I guess she didn't want me to be an absentee father like Keisha's dad was.

"Nine months later, we had Simone. She was the most beautiful baby girl you would have ever seen. Light brown eyes like her momma, and the fairest skin

I'd ever seen on any baby. You would have thought she was white when she came out but no, that was my blood. My daughter!" Lenny beamed with pride.

"Keisha's momma lived with us up until Simone was born then she left with her boyfriend to Vegas, I think. Guess she didn't want to raise any grandchildren, so Keisha and I raised Simone alone in their small two-bedroom apartment. I got a job at the local fast-food restaurant and made barely enough to keep the lights on. Keisha had never worked before and didn't want a job so we agreed that she would stay home and take care of Simone and for the longest time, she did it well. But things changed when Simone became a teenager.

"We needed more money and Keisha still refused to get a job, so we fought a lot. Sometimes we didn't know it, but Simone watched us fight. I wanted to be a good father and keep her away from everything I grew up around, but Keisha made it hard. Simone started lying to us, sneaking out of the house, and even started getting into fights at school. She started hanging out with the wrong crowds and I know if we'd done more, we could have prevented this, but Keisha refused to accept that she was the problem. I worked all day to provide, and she couldn't even take care of our daughter. I started to blame her for Simone's issues.

"I'm not sure how it happened because she was too scared to tell us until it was too late, but Simone got pregnant. She used to wear baggy clothes and we thought it was a phase she was going through until I saw she was showing. She was six months pregnant, and Keisha didn't even notice. Six months! I had to find out by how she dressed and avoided us.

"Well after that, Keisha and I tried to keep things cordial for Simone and the baby's sake. We had a grandchild on the way and the last thing Simone needed was the stress of us fighting. Imagine that. My baby was having a baby."

Lenny paused and closed his eyes as Oliver stared.

"Lenny? You okay?"

"Yeah…sorry. Simone died the day she had Bastian…" He froze again and cleared his throat. "No parent should have to bury their child. The pain. I can't describe it. I felt empty. Like I failed. I've been failing my whole life, but this felt worse than all my other failures. The doctors said her body was too weak to make it through the delivery and just like that, she was gone. There we were, Keisha and I with a grandson and no daughter."

There was another pause.

"Remember how I said much is taken from those to whom things are given? I felt like this was a similar exchange to what happened with Rahzmel and my grandmother. The trade-off for one was the other.

"Well anyway, guess the pain of everything ended up being too much for Keisha cause shortly after Simone died, Keisha disappeared. Vanished. She was gone and I was left with Bastian. I was all alone with a baby. Every time I looked at him, I told myself I could never leave him like Keisha did."

"She just up and left? How could she do that to you and her grandson?"

"I'm not sure but I didn't fight it much. Truth be told, I'd been abandoned for most of my life, and this was just another person gone. Keisha disappeared and I decided to not fight it or go after her. Even though I knew I was going to have to do it alone, I convinced myself it was for the best. After what happened to Simone, I didn't want Bastian to fall down the same path his mother did. I wanted things to be different for him. I needed to break that little boy from the cycle we've all been living through even if it meant giving up everything I had. Like my grandmother did for me."

"And like my mother did for me," Oliver responded.

"Your mother?"

"Yeah, Lenny. My story's been interesting since you've been gone but in short, I got adopted by the best woman I have ever known; Mabel-Ara Burke. I hear so many similarities between her and your grandmother. I'd like to tell you about her if I can."

"Yes. I'd like that."

CHAPTER 22:

SEE HER WHEN I DREAM

Oliver Burke

"Well I know all about the house fire, Rahzmel dying, and why they were in that uppity neighborhood in Brooklyn that day. I know it because I *was* there too."

"What?!? You were there?" Lenny interrupted choking on the smoke departing past his lips. "But no one knew anything about any Oliver Mahlah."

"Yes, I was there and the *'no survivors'* Mr. Green told you about was my family. Jeremiah, Isaac, Lillian Evie, Tonisha, and Mabel-Ara. That was my family."

Oliver rubbed the permanent burn scar on his tricep as he spoke about the fire. He watched as Lenny's attention turned from the lake to his blemish, then to his eyes.

"That came from the fire, didn't it?" Lenny asked pointing to the burn mark.

Embarrassed, Oliver went to roll his sleeve down, but Lenny stopped him. "No, don't. If anyone can relate, it's me," he traded scratching the thin scar beneath his lips. His voice was thick with empathy. "That attack I told you about from my first night in jail. Yeah, I still have this little baby to remember it."

They sat silent, both at a loss for words as they attempted to process things.

"After you disappeared, I went looking for you, Lenny. We used to do everything together and I couldn't believe you would have left just like that. I knew something was wrong and ended up at the Clubhouse. I know you told me not to, but I felt I had no other options."

Lenny shook his head. "I knew taking you there that day was a bad idea. I didn't see it until it was too late."

"Deep down, I blamed you for taking me there. I blamed you for disappearing. Most of all, I blamed you for giving me a tiny bit of happiness and then taking it away."

"It was never my intention."

"I know but I still blamed you because it was easy to blame someone else and that's when everything went downhill for me. That was the day I first got involved with Rahzmel's gang and things began to spiral out of my control."

Lenny held confusion in his stare. "When I checked on you, it sounded like things were going okay."

"It wasn't until Rahzmel began to ask me for things. Just like he did for you until you were in jail. Like you, I ended up going to prison for being at the wrong place at the wrong time. Just like you."

"Which prison did they send you to and why?"

"Same prison as you from the sounds of it. Port Authority Corrections Center. I must have gotten there after you left." He stared at his friend with absolution painted in his glare. "I got arrested for being at a murder scene. They connected me with being there because I left a backpack but, I didn't do anything. It was Rahzmel and the others who did everything.

"My time in prison was like yours and when I got out, I didn't go back to Rahzmel. I found a home and started my new life. That's where Mabel-Ara adopted me and gave me a family."

Oliver saw Lenny's attention was now fixed on him and smiled and continued.

"I was taken in by the greatest woman I ever knew, Mabel-Ara Burke. We used to call her Ma. She cared for me and on the day she officially adopted me… on my eighteenth birthday… Rahzmel tried to kill us all. He came for me because I didn't come back to his stupid gang when I got out. He, Croc, and the others tried to kill me, but they didn't succeed." Oliver paused and watched Lenny's surprise. "They all burned with my family in the house but… I got out. My mom helped me through a window in the basement and she stayed to make sure Rahzmel didn't get out. I lost everything in that fire…"

There was another pause and Oliver watched as Lenny wiped the corners of his eyes. He could see his friend was connecting with the story.

"Oliver…I didn't know. I tried calling you when I was in prison to tell you to be careful but when I called the number I was given, Rah picked up. That was the day I realized how much control he still had over me and that he abandoned me."

"Yeah, I never knew you tried until now."

Lenny held disbelief in his look.

"I should've listened to you that day when you told me not to go back to the clubhouse, Lenny. I was lost when you disappeared. You were the only friend I had… my best friend and I got sucked into Rahzmel's manipulative ways. Could hear it now—the venom that has always lived beneath his empty promises. I didn't truly see it until the day I got to PACC but that was the day that I realized I was a prisoner long before I arrived at the jail. Just like you."

"I regretted that day for the last thirty years," Lenny exchanged as he wiped his eyes every few seconds. "I don't know why I took you there. I think I was trying to seem cool to get you to like me but didn't realize what I was doing. I barely understood things, myself."

"You were my best friend and I loved you. Rahzmel did this to both of us."

Oliver shook his head in understanding so Lenny continued. "What happened after the fire?"

"After she was killed, I couldn't stay in Brooklyn anymore, so I left for Chicago, where I spent almost twenty years. I only moved back recently and got a new life with Amerie. I could barely recognize Brooklyn when I got back."

Lenny threw his cigarette into the lake and turned to his friend. He had a curious look on his face and Oliver could tell he was treasuring their time together. "What was Mabel-Ara like?"

Oliver smiled brightly as happiness settled in his soul. "Unlike anyone I've ever met before," Oliver admitted with a wistful smile. "She had a personality that always made you feel protected in her presence. Like there was always this layer of safety. She wasn't a cup-half-full type of person. With her, it was always full. Overflowing even. In the moments of distress, she never made it seem like it emptied. She never let you see her sorrows or disappointments. It's funny, she used to say we were what she dreamed of. I never told her that I used to dream about her when I was at the orphanage. I would see her when I closed my eyes. Still do."

There was another pause as Oliver caught himself getting choked up. "She had a slow walk and small hunch, but you can tell she was youthful and vibrant in her heyday. Her smile. Oh, man. Her smile was the brightest and lit up even the darkest moods. Although it came often, I remember she had tiredness to her smile which I knew was from always using it to make others feel better. When she spoke, nothing else mattered. She told stories of her past and even the smallest details had your undivided attention. She had others, like me, and they were all my family. It's funny. I used to tell people she was my father because I didn't want people's sympathy. You know. The sympathy that came from people thinking you were a little black boy without a dad. Now when I think back on it, I'm embarrassed but wasn't wrong. She was everything."

"That's beautiful, man. You were an orphan, and you got a family. You used to be so angry all the time and I didn't think that anger would ever go away but it did. It sounds like she helped you. She sounds like a special lady. Someone very important to you. Like my grandmama…"

Oliver smiled at his friend's understanding.

"Lenny… It sounds like there were a lot of similarities between her and your grandma. They both loved us and were taken by Rahzmel, and…" He paused and placed one hand on Lenny's shoulder. "…although we haven't seen each other, I feel like we've been connected somehow through all of this. Even though we've been apart in distance, we've been together all along. Even though everything in this world was against you, you did your best. We both did."

"My best was never enough. When my grandmama passed, life only got harder. It's funny how before you asked me if I 'got time.' The irony of it is I don't have much of it left at all. I'm not sure if you've been able to tell but I'm sick. In fact, I'm dying. Stage IV lung cancer…"

Oliver looked at the cigarette in Lenny's hand and then back to his eyes. Their eyes connected before Lenny smiled and continued.

"I know what you're thinking. Why's this guy smoking when he has cancer? My time for treatment is long gone, my friend. At this point, I'm simply trying to enjoy the days I have left. Frankly, cigarettes are a part of what still brings me joy. That and my grandson."

On his face, Oliver could see a look of concession. Of resignation. "How much longer do you have?"

"I'm not sure but I couldn't go without first finding you. For thirty years I thought about asking for your forgiveness and thought I missed the chance. Now that you're here, I can finally say… I'm sorry."

Lenny could no longer hold his heartbreak as he fell to his knees in a disheveled heap. His grief poured down his face in a flood of uncontrollable tears as he pled to Oliver's feet. "I'm so sorry I should've done more to help you. You didn't deserve that, and I put you in that life. That was my cousin and deep down I knew what he was, but you didn't. When I was locked up, it was like I was watching you make the same mistakes I made and there was nothing I could do. Through it all, the worst part wasn't losing my freedom. It was realizing I never had any."

Oliver stood lost for words. He sympathized with his friend and could hear the wounds in his story. He knew there was sadness but was surprised when he didn't see any fear in Lenny's face. "Are you afraid? Are you scared to go?"

"No…no…no… I'm happy to go. I've lived life the best way I could, and it's brought me acceptance for everything. Even though there were hard parts, my life's been incredible. I never really had much but always felt like I had enough, and I'm good with that."

At that moment, Oliver also began tearing up as he slowly raised Lenny from the ground and held his friend. Through his touch, he could now feel the deep emotional wounds that Lenny was finally releasing through their conversation and held him tight. He felt Lenny's shoulders drop in resignation which freed the tension he knew was there. He'd noticed the conflict in Lenny had faded and for the first time since they'd reconnected, he sensed his friend felt "free."

He finally seems comfortable. Lenny's recount of his life showed his perils and Oliver sheepishly admitted his error.

"You have nothing to apologize for. I decided to go to the clubhouse that day and started hanging with Rahzmel, not you. I thought I was angry at you for leaving but deep down inside, I was angry at myself for thinking that life was for me. I gave up *everything*, including my childhood, not you. I want you to know that there's nothing for you to be sorry for. I did that to myself."

"I lost my childhood too, Oliver, and don't want the same for my grandson," he started softly, avoiding his eyes. "I don't have much longer and don't want to send him to a group home or put him into a foster program. You and I both know what programs like that do to children. He deserves a better childhood than we had. I've heard about what you've been doing at the youth center and know it needs to be you. Besides my grandmama, you were the only other person I could ever fully trust. Before and after my time with you, I could never relax and be myself. When I was with you, I didn't feel like I needed to be a gangster. I felt sheltered."

"Wait...Lenny... what are you saying?"

"I'm saying...no wait...I'm begging you...please give Bastian a life we never had. Give him a life with someone who cares for him. Someone who will show him right from wrong and will protect him. We lost our youth and had to grow up too quickly. That boy deserves more. Please, Oliver. Please take care of him."

"Wow..." Oliver froze. "You want me to be his guardian? Like... for real? That's a lot to take in."

"I know man, but it *has* to be you. You've been doing really great things. If something like that youth center was around when we were teens, things would have been different. *We* would've been different. In my heart, I feel it has to be you."

"I wouldn't even know where to begin. Plus, I would have to run it by Amerie. We don't have any kids of our own."

"I get it. I don't know how much time I have so please let me know as soon as possible. Speak to Amerie and give me a call."

There was a pause so Lenny could catch his breath before he continued. "I never thought I wanted to be a parent until I became one. Once I did, I thanked God every day for choosing me. I used to dream about one day seeing this type of joy. From my darkest days in the coldest cell, I had hoped for some reprieve at the end of it all and, honestly, I thought it was going to be my death but was wrong…this is it. When I first held that beautiful boy, nothing else mattered. Not poverty, not jail, not losing my grandmother. The most important thing in my life at that moment was that baby in my palms. And through it all, I could've been scared but surprisingly, I wasn't. I was honored he chose me. Please talk to Amerie and let me know. Please?"

Lenny then turned his attention to the park and yelled out. "Yo Bas, it's getting dark. Let's get outta here. Let's go home."

Although he wanted to protect his grandson from the perils he knew would face as a black man in America, Lenny also didn't want to rob Bastian of his innocence any sooner than he needed to. The boy was jubilant, and Lenny was certain the truths about his life and past would haunt the adolescent the way Lenny was haunted.

Instead, Lenny spoke to him about cartoons and action heroes. He spoke to him about his favorite cereal brands and who his best friends were at that time. He spoke to him about his occupational desires for when he grew up—which was a superhero for most of his childhood until he was six years old and then wanted to be a firefighter. Bastian held bravery that Lenny didn't have at his age and Lenny stood utterly impressed at how mature he was.

Through it all, Lenny knew his number one obligation was to protect Bastian by any means possible. He didn't have much but was ready to trade it all if it meant his grandson would have the advantages in life he never had. His unvoiced past was one he couldn't bring himself to tell. He wanted Bastian to have a clean slate and formulate his own bias and relationships and knew it would come from him being guided but not misled. He didn't want to manipulate him with talks of his past and the causes that affected everything he'd become. The past that bridged his story with Oliver's and was the formation of everything they'd become. This is why it had to be Oliver.

CHAPTER 23:

A PLACE WE CAN CALL HOME

Oliver Burke

When Oliver arrived home that evening, Amerie was sitting on the couch eating ice cream and watching her favorite show, Grey's Anatomy. She'd always enjoyed the drama and looked up as Oliver approached to kiss her forehead. He wore a pensive expression on his face and she could tell his mind was conflicted. Once she switched the television off, she turned her body towards his.

"Hi, baby – What's up? How'd it go with Lenny?"

"Hi, honey – It was okay," he replied shortly.

Oliver knew she was looking for more, but he struggled to provide it. *What can I say? How will she react? She was already against this from the start. This won't help.* He began to sweat nervously as a sudden rush of emotion erupted in his being. He tried to find the right words to describe his conundrum but couldn't, so she continued.

"Babe – You okay? What's wrong?"

Oliver wiped the sweat from his forehead and walked over to the thermostat to check if it was working properly. "Is this thing broken? How's it so hot and this reads 70 degrees?"

"It's working fine. It's you who's not talking. What happened?"

Oliver exhaled and looked at her as she walked over and used a napkin to wipe his face.

"I thought I had it bad," he began slowly, "but he had it just as bad, maybe even worse."

Oliver paused again. He wrapped his arms around himself and glanced around the room—refusing to make eye contact. He felt an overwhelming level of embarrassment for the anger he'd previously held towards his friend, which paired with the sudden ball of sadness resting in the back of his throat.

"I learned that he's sick, uh, he's dying. Dementia, I think. Wait. Or maybe pneumonia. No, it was Parkinson's. Yeah, I think Parkinson's. Oh, wait-"

Amerie interrupted, "Oliver?" She sensed he was struggling and grabbed his trembling shoulders. "Babe, what's going on? You're shaking. You can talk to me."

She squeezed him tight until his trembling and breathing slowed.

"He didn't seem all right. Lenny. He seemed...sad. Like heartbroken. Not from his illness but it felt like he was sad about something else. Turns out he's actually dying from cancer."

How do I tell her? Oliver thought to himself. *She was already against me calling him back. How do I tell her he's dying and needs me right now? I don't even know if I want to become a parent. Now I need to ask her to be one? Is that selfish of me?*

"Oliver! Please talk to me!"

"It's Lenny. It's our conversation. I have something to tell you."

"What's wrong? You're scaring me."

He watched as she placed her hands over his to slow the trembling.

He started slow. "Lenny said he came back to find me. He asked me. Uh. He asked *us* if we would be able to take his grandson, Bastian."

207

"Wait, what? Really? Take him like adopt him?" Her shock was glaring, and he wanted to stop but knew he had to get everything out, so he continued.

"Yeah, that was my reaction also. I didn't say yes or anything. Told him I would speak with you."

"But why you? You haven't seen this guy for nearly thirty years, and he shows up outta nowhere to ask you to take his grandson? I knew something was off about this whole thing."

"Yeah. I found it weird too, but it didn't seem like he was trying to pawn this kid off to someone else. I felt what he was going through. I felt it deeply actually. He spoke in a way that described the many similarities in our stories. I didn't want to bring it up to you because I know you were against me calling him in the first place."

They both sat in silence, deliberating on the revelation. Oliver watched as the shock in her face softened and turned to compassion before Amerie found her voice.

"Well, you know I never wanted to be a parent. If I were to become one, I can't imagine my first child not being birthed by me."

Oliver shook his head in understanding. He also never saw himself as a parent and thought back to the struggles he'd encountered as a child.

I barely had a childhood; how can I be a parent now? Even worse, how can I force this on Amerie?

"Was there no one else who could take care of him?" She started slowly. "Lenny didn't have anyone else?"

"It didn't sound like he really had anyone else."

"I don't think we should do this."

"Okay but think about this. If we don't bring that little boy home, he'll probably go into the system and may get adopted quickly or may stay in for a bit." He rubbed his eyes nervously and scratched his head as he went on. "He'll probably think about Lenny every day and wonder why he left him. As he grows up, he may begin to understand, or he may grow up resentful and angry. Like I did when I was younger…"

Oliver watched as Amerie stared as he spoke and thought back to his own time in the foster care system. *How can I send this kid to that? How can I abandon him when I have a chance to change things for him?* Amerie continued.

"But if we bring him into our home, our life will change," she remarked slowly to limit any agitation from coming through in her tone. "We'd be responsible for another life and cannot move around how we move around now. We'd first need to learn how to take care of a child. How old did you say he was?"

"I think he's seven or eight years old."

"Okay, so he's not a baby. That's a plus. He's still young, and families like kids that young."

"So, you're saying send him into the system?" Oliver questioned in disappointment.

She remained quiet while deliberating so he interjected. "If we do it right, we can mold him, nurture him, and show him that there are *good* people who still care for him just like his grandpa does." He saw he had her complete attention and continued. "Do you think we can do it?"

"I don't know, babe. It's a huge responsibility and I work so much right now."

"Well, I'm not working right now. I can even bring him by the youth center and introduce him to Jalacie and some of the other kids."

"It sounds like you're leaning towards a yes?"

"Well...Ummm...no. I'm just weighing our options," he admitted. "I know first-hand how real it gets in the foster care system and I don't know how I'd sleep every night knowing I sent Bastian to that when I could have changed things for him."

"How *we* could have changed things for him. This affects both of us."

"Yes, I know," he looked at her apologetically. He expected her to get upset and was surprised when she continued with her coldness instead.

"I can't decide for you, but I think I'm leaning towards a no. Frankly, I don't have the time and want to be realistic. You know Lenny so maybe you can talk to him to see if there are any better options? If there are, maybe we can consider those? What do you think?"

"I think I need to sleep on it. I'll call Lenny back and ask if he has someone else."

"And if he doesn't?"

"Then I don't know, babe. I have time right now and can be there for Bastian. I'm not working and think we can do it."

"Are you serious?" She began. "That's incredibly selfish of you. Your volunteerism at the youth center is admirable but it doesn't bring any money. I work long hours and will now need to take care of two of you? I can't believe you."

She began to storm out of the room and just before she slammed the door, Oliver made one final remark.

"I won't force you to do this, Amerie. I'm just going to go to the hospital and I'll figure it out."

*****

That night, as he slept on the couch, Oliver's racing mind drifted back to a place where he hadn't found himself in many years. He was conflicted over his friend's sudden reappearance and his pending decision on Bastian's future and turned to the one place he could count on to reveal the truths he hid from himself—his dreams.

In this particular dream, he watched himself as a teenager on the day of his release from prison. He stood in the large doorway of the once unfamiliar edifice he grew to call home and felt goosebumps on his forearms. In the scene, Officers Jefferson and his partner Officer Smith were standing beside him as they waited for the door to open, and he knew this was no dream at all. The familiarity of the scene replayed one of his fondest memories and he recognized the significance of this. It was not meaningless or random like most dreams. He thought to himself, *this is the day I got out of jail and was taken to Mabel-Ara's house. On the first day, I was able to relax and feel comfortable.*

Seeing the determination and genuine care in the officer's faces reminded him of the comfort he had in their presence that day. Although he never admitted it to them, he was scared, and they helped quell that fear. They turn his fear into a genuine curiosity at all the possibilities of what could be. His first thought was what could be waiting behind the large door. The officers knew and Oliver was forever grateful that they decided to take a chance on a damaged, misplaced teen.

Although they originated as strangers by circumstance, he was happy that they stuck around when others didn't and became family by choice.

As he watched the scene unfold, Oliver could see the anger in the face of his younger self and stood embarrassed. He knew this masked his rooted fear and the desperation he had of wishing for a place to belong. This was right after he'd been released from Port Authority Correction Center after serving close to 24 months for unlawful gun possession. After his release, he had no idea where he would end up next and remembered being uneasy. He was terrified and suddenly recalled how anxious he felt waiting for the door to open. His anxiety was palpable.

When the door finally opened, all the same emotions he felt that day suddenly reappeared as he looked at Ma and felt chills. She opened the door with a warm smile, which he'd grown to love, and her dirty apron which was his reminder that this was the first time he tried her meatloaf. He remembered the apprehension he felt seeing her pale white skin and stood embarrassed.

In his dream, his witnessing-self stood at the end of the stone walkway that led to the front door so he could not hear their dialogue but remembered every word spoken. It was as if he'd re-lived that day multiple times before this flashback and this was another reenactment.

"Are you hungry? You look hungry. I just finished making dinner so come eat," he recited, silently mimicking Mabel-Ara's words.

As the scene continued, Oliver watched as the group made their way to the dining room, where everyone was seated and dinner was being served. He saw his siblings and smiled at the pure joy and innocence on their faces. *I miss them so much*, he thought as he traded his attention between each of them before finally landing on his older adopted brother, Jeremiah, who looked at the displaced teenager in front of him. He watched the ear-to-ear smile that his adoptive brother displayed and could see his dimples piercing his pudgy cheeks. It was a sight that he could never forget. He then remembered how confused he was that day at the size of Jeremiah's afro and giggled.

Man, I miss you.

When he looked up, he saw Ma leaving the room and turned his attention to follow her into the kitchen. He recalled the smell that filled the dining room that day and how it had tapped into pleasure senses he hadn't used before. The aroma alone brought him curiosity that turned to excitement when he entered the kitchen and found its source.

He stared as Ma finished with her final preparations of the meatloaf. He had never tasted real meatloaf before, and this smell was vastly different from the meatloaf they served in prison.

At that moment, he was craving her touch more than anything he'd ever wanted before and reached his hand out—begging to steal a moment where he could feel her soft embrace one more time.

Unfortunately, this dream was a one-way visit, and he knew she could not hear or feel his witnessing-self but still tried in hopes of finding favor on his side. *If I only had one more day with you...*

He grinned and watched as she gathered her piping hot dish from the kitchen stove to take it to the dining room table. At the moment that she disappeared back through the swinging doors, he followed her through and woke up. He exhaled a big sigh of satisfaction because he knew these moments didn't come often and took it as a sign. He smiled at the thought of Mabel-Ara. His angel.

*****

That afternoon, Oliver attempted to call Lenny to inquire further if he had anyone else to watch Bastian. He hadn't heard from Lenny since their meeting in the park roughly two days earlier and grew curious.

It sounded like there was an urgency before. I'm surprised he hasn't called and texted me.

At his first attempt at calling Lenny, his friend did not pick up so he left it as is—assuming he would call back later that day—but he never did. He checked his phone regularly and even made test calls to ensure he still had phone service, but Lenny never called. He tried him back one more time before going to bed and when his friend did not pick up, Oliver began to worry.

By the next morning, Oliver rolled over to see that Lenny still hadn't returned his call and grew further concerned. This was beginning to feel oddly familiar to when they were teenagers and Oliver had the same uneasiness.

Where is he? I hope he's not in trouble again.

He remembered how this unease had caused his teenage self to make one of the worst decisions he'd ever made in his life. A decision that led him into the care of a ruthless drug dealer while searching for his missing friend. He tried Lenny again but this time, decided to leave a voicemail when he didn't pick up.

"Hey, Lenny – Calling you *again*. I'm getting worried. Call me back when you see this."

Almost instantly after he hung up the voicemail, Oliver felt his phone vibrating on his hip. When he looked, he saw Lenny's number and quickly picked it up.

Finally, he thought.

"Hello…hello…Lenny?"

"Yes, Oliver. It's me," he said softly. "Sorry I missed your call. How are you?"

"I'm good, Lenny. Haven't heard from you. Where have you been? Are you okay?"

Oliver could hear Lenny's dry cough through the phone receiver which was followed by him blowing his nose. He cleared his throat and then continued.

"I'm not doing well, man. I've been in the hospital. I don't remember much but do recall how I was feeling dizzy then woke up in this hospital. Doctors have been monitoring me since."

"In the hospital? Which hospital are you in? I'm on the way."

"I'm at NYC Health in Harlem. I'd love to see you. Bas is here with me. He's such a big boy. He called 911 when I collapsed and has been here with me since. Did you and Amerie talk about that thing we spoke about?"

"Yes, Lenny, we did…let's talk more when I get there."

"Okay. That sounds good."

Oliver could then hear Lenny turn his attention away from the phone receiver as he spoke to someone in his room.

"Bas, remember my *best* friend, Oliver? He's coming to visit us." There was a pause before Lenny came back on the line. "Thank you, Oliver. I'm in room 302. Please hurry. See you soon, my friend."

"Take care of yourself. I'm on the way. Please hold on until I get there."

"I'll try…"

CHAPTER 24:

MOSTLY ABOUT A MONSTER

Oliver Burke

When Oliver finally arrived at the hospital that afternoon, he felt chills. He wore his nervousness like a mask and could tell the nurses saw his anguish as he walked the halls on the 3rd floor. He wasn't sure what condition he was going to find his friend in but believed he needed to be by his side. Their reconciliation hit him hard but he knew Lenny was dealing in ways he could never understand. As he approached room 302, he inhaled to put on a brave face and walked through the door.

When he entered, Oliver was shocked at how cold the room felt. Not cold in the literal sense but the metaphorical sense. The room felt lifeless and barren as if he was standing in a tomb. At one end laid Lenny with Bastian sitting by his bedside holding his hand. Oliver could tell he was close to death and got choked up as he observed the saline tubs connected to his veins. Both of their attention turned as Oliver slowly approached his bedside.

"Oliver, you made it," he remarked sickly. "Thanks for coming. Bas, say hi to Oliver."

"Hi, Oliver."

"Hey Bas, good to see you again. Are those your coloring books over there on the table? You like superheroes?"

"Yes. My favorite is the Black Panther. He's like me."

217

"Oh yeah?" Oliver replied looking at Lenny with an encouraging smile. "Because you're both brave right?"

"Yep and the Black Panther is the king of Wakanda. He saves everyone."

"That's great. Sounds *just* like you, Bas. You'll have to tell me the story sometime. Would that be okay?"

"Sure!" Bastian remarked excitedly.

Lenny smiled at the exchange and when Oliver turned his attention back to his friend, he watched as Lenny began to doze off as the heart monitor began beeping.

"Wait…what's happening," Oliver questioned looking around. "Lenny! Lenny! Help! Someone help us! Please help him!"

Bastian stood confused and slowly backed away from the bedside as four members of the hospital staff rushed into the room and quickly scanned Lenny's body. "He's not breathing. We need to perform CPR. Get the cart in here!"

One of the nurses backed Oliver away from Lenny's bedside as the doctor locked his elbows, clamped his hands together, and began chest compressions. "Four milligrams of epi," the doctor yelled.

"Grandpa! What's happening?" Bastian cried out. Oliver tried to shield him from the scene, but Bastian fought through. "Grandpa!"

"He's still in v-fib. Charge up the defibrillator. Now! We need to shock!"

"Charging it 200."

"Grandpa!"

"Someone get that kid out of here!"

"Help him! Please! Help him!" Oliver cried out. "Please!"

"Sir, we're doing all we can but need you to leave. Now!"

One of the nurses pushed Oliver and Bastian out of the room as the doctor was receiving the defibrillator paddles. As he exited, Oliver gave one final look back.

"Clear!"

*****

As minutes passed, Oliver continued to stand with Bastian as they impatiently waited for updates. They could still hear the beeping from outside of the room until after a few moments, it stopped.

Oh no...

One of the nurses came out of the room in a melancholy manner and before she could say anything, Oliver looked her in the face and erupted.

"No... nooo...Lenny," Oliver cried out. "Lenny please! Please...c'mon man...please!"

Still unsure exactly what was happening, Bastian also erupted in tears and attempted to run into the hospital room, but the nurse stood in his way and stopped him. In that same minute, two of the doctors rushed Lenny out of the room and down the hall as another came out to speak with Oliver.

"Sir...can we speak?"

Oliver felt numb and allowed the doctor to walk him to the side.

"Is that your friend?"

With his voice shaking Oliver replied, "that's my brother."

"Your brother's stable but suffered a major heart attack. We're monitoring him but he can't speak."

"Wait…what? What does that mean? Is he okay?"

The same doctor looked at the nurse beside him. "Please watch the boy."

"There were some complications from cancer and your brother had a massive heart attack. We almost lost him but he's a fighter. He's barely conscious now and cannot speak. We're doing all we can, but I don't know how much longer he has."

Oliver's heart skipped and his stomach was in knots. "What does that mean?"

"I should know more soon. For now, is there somewhere for you and the boy to go?"

"We're not going anywhere. We'll be waiting right here."

"Okay."

*****

After the hospital staff left Oliver and Bastian returned to the room. He wanted to be there when Lenny returned and sat with the confused child. He was still processing the scene and knew Bastian was also, and watched as he wiped his eyes every few seconds. Oliver looked over, still lost for words, placing a hand on Bastian's shoulder in comfort.

What can I say? There's no one here to take care of him and he just watched his grandfather suffer a heart attack. What can I say?

"Hey Bas," he choked out. "It's going to be okay. They're working on your grandpa. He's going to be okay."

"But what happened?"

"The doctors are still figuring it out but they're the best doctors here and will do everything they can for him."

"What if he doesn't come back? Like Mommy…"

Oliver stood frozen with his stomach still in knots. The heaviness of the scene and the thought of what came next struck him deeply. He couldn't imagine Lenny dying so soon after their reconciliation. He had no answer and struggled to find the right words.

I need to do something. I need to take both of our minds off this. It just isn't fair. He shouldn't have to deal with this.

"Your grandpa's going to be okay. We need to pray for him. He's going to be just fine," he said in a tone as if he was also trying to assure himself. "Remember how you said the Black Panther saves everyone?"

"Yes."

"Well let's do like the Black Panther and pray for grandpa. He needs us."

Oliver could tell he still had Bastian's attention and continued.

"Hey, Bas, while we wait for grandpa to come back, how about a story?"

"Story about what?"

"Well…it's kind of a story about a boy…and also about a prince. But mostly about a monster…"

CHAPTER 25:

THE PRINCE & PETER PT. 1

Oliver Burke

*T*he story begins a long, long time ago in a large village called Brockland. The village was the wealthiest in the land and housed about a thousand villagers, most of whom knew each other on a first-name basis or by the title of their job, such as the carpenter, the butcher, the librarian, etcetera, etcetera. It was very close to other similarly sized villages in the area which all bordered Brockland in every direction. The village was pretty well maintained and most villagers had a job to do to keep it going. What made the village exceptionally special was the fact that it was also the home to the previous King and Queen of the land, who now lived a life in solitude after losing one of their children a year earlier. The present King and Queen lived in another village.

There was one boy named Peter who was from one of the smaller neighboring villages. He was smart and had lots of heart, but he was always left out and pushed away by the other kids in his village. Like an outcast.

"Why were the kids mean to Peter?" Bastian questioned.

"Well…that's just what kids are like sometimes… adults are like that too until they learn better. Have you ever met people like that?"

"Yes – I have but what happened next? What happened to Peter?"

Oliver was happy to see he still had Bastian's undivided attention because it meant for that moment, that his mind wasn't on Lenny. He continued.

One day, Peter showed up at the field in hopes of joining their game. He watched and watched as the team captains selected their players until it was just him left. He looked around and saw he was once again passed over. 'Please…choose me,' Peter begged them. 'For anything. It doesn't matter what, please just let me be a part of a team. Please I want to play…'

Unfortunately, his plea failed, and the others giggled as they ran off to play their game. Peter stood there on the verge of tears at the fact that he was once again left on the sidelines with his pride deflated and his spirits crushed. Everyone else had size, strength, speed, and some form of wealth, but he was left with only his intelligence—a currency they believed brought no value to their games.

For the longest time, he'd become used to their treatment and grew numb to it, but this day was different. This day hit him hard. He was embarrassed and did his best to fight back his tears and sorrow.

"Why didn't they choose him?" Bastian questioned with a concerning undertone. "Why did they always leave him out of their games."

"It's because they thought he was different. He wasn't like them, and they couldn't see his potential."

"Different? Because he was smart and poor?"

"Well …sort of. He didn't have all the physical things they all had, and they were afraid. It was horrible but stick with me. We're going to learn a lot more and the rest of the story will reveal everything."

"Okay!"

So, because Peter had become numb to the treatment he'd experienced up until that point, he somewhat expected it but was hoping that day would be different. What the other kids did not know was Peter's grandfather, who was his guardian, was very sick. The town's doctor had come to visit them earlier that day and informed them that there was nothing he could do for the old man without some form of money. He diagnosed that the old man's body was reacting to a rare poison and the only thing that could heal him was more of the same type of poison, which they did not keep in the village. They would need to pay the doctor to secure the poison from another village, which he could tell would be a difficult task for the young man and his ailing grandfather. Due to that, the doctor recommended they make the old man's last few days comfortable.

So, when Peter went to the field that day, he was looking for a distraction. Reassurance that things would work out and he would be fine, but he didn't find it. He was simply reminded how cruel the world was and that he would soon be all alone.

Heartbroken and disappointed, Peter packed up a knapsack and blindly ran into the local forest distraught and in tears. He ran, and ran, and ran until he hit a dead end and realized he couldn't run any longer. When he wiped his eyes and looked up, he was staring into the entrance of a dark cave with what looked like ashes and bones all over. The cave was gloomy, and he was afraid but when he turned around and looked behind him, all he could think about was the other kids who treated him poorly and his dying grandfather. He was sad and thought there was nothing for him back home. Nothing but grief, cruelty, and the forthcoming loss.

He also thought about how others viewed him as weak and small and knew they would not treat him fairly until he forced them to. Gave them a reason to respect him.

In his search, Peter also hoped he would find something that could help save his grandfather. To him, his entire being was riding on his bravery so he decided to go on. He was desperate and proceeded forward until he disappeared into the darkness of the cave.

"Was he scared?"

"Yeah – he was very scared but didn't think he had any other choice. The others back in the village didn't accept him and he didn't know how to help his grandfather. There were very few people who treated him like a human being and one of them was dying. He had no time to be afraid."

So, Peter walked and walked until he finally found a large room with a fire burning in the center of it. The dimly lit space was warm, and the fire seemed fresh. He began to think he was not alone but slowly continued forward anyway. As he walked, he saw the room was filled with gold everywhere and became even more frightened. He knew this gold could help his grandfather but as he continued further, he worried about the true cost of it. He could not believe so much gold would sit unattended like this and grew anxious that he was not alone.

When he finally got to the fire in the center of the room, he looked to his right and saw nothing but darkness. He then looked to his left assuming he would see the same, but he was wrong. At that moment, he caught his eyes with something in the dark. The eyes he saw did not mirror his own and were reptilian with a vertical slit for the pupil. As he stood there frozen, the eyes grew larger and began to rise with his fear. He could not move and simply stood there as the figure approached swiftly and loudly until it towered directly over him.

"What was it?" Bastian questioned eagerly before Oliver continued.

Peter could barely believe it. He'd only heard stories of dragons and knew they had a reputation for being cruel and mean. He watched as the dragon extended its wings to their full length and shot fire into the air flaring the entire cave in heat and ember. He was petrified and knew he should've run but didn't. He had no friends back at home, his grandfather was almost gone, and he couldn't think of any reason not to let the dragon take his life.

The dragon saw this and retracted its wings and motioned right in front of Peter. He was so close that Peter could feel the heat radiating from the dragon's scales. The dragon stared back square into Peter's eyes but did not see the same fear he'd seen in the others. To the dragon, this boy seemed different, and the dragon grew curious about this mysterious visitor. It continued to stare and simply breathed through its wide nostrils while it waited for the slightest bit of fear from Peter, but that fear did not come.

The dragon finally realized this boy was different from the others who attempted to steal its gold and grew further intrigued by its mysterious visitor. Seconds after the stare-down began, the dragon took two steps back and finally spoke.

"Boy…why do you not run. I can scorch your body in seconds with a cough or a sneeze, or rip you into pieces with one clench of my jaw upon your warm flesh yet you don't run in fear? Why?"

Peter could barely believe it. First, he walked into a dark cave, now he was standing toe-to-toe with a fire-breathing dragon who talked, and he barely wince. He couldn't think of a logical explanation for it and responded with the first thing that came to his mind.

"I don't mean to bother you, dragon. I've gotten lost and accidentally wandered into your lair. I simply want to make my way back and I'll leave you alone."

The dragon watched Peter's lips as he spoke and saw as his eyes traded from his own to the gold and back. It believed it found the boy's motive for his intrusion and continued.

"I usually don't let intruders or robbers leave my home alive, boy. Why do you think no one has told the village people about me or my presence here? It's because no one has lived to speak on what they've seen."

"I'm sorry, dragon," Peter responded nervously. "I mean you no offense by my intrusion and had no plans to rob or harm

you," he lied. "I simply got lost and should be going now. I won't say anything about what I've seen here. You can trust me."

"Wait, boy," the dragon demanded with a conviction in its voice that shook the room. "I will give you a chance to leave with all the gold you desire if, and only if, you can best me in a contest of wits. If you get one of my three questions correct, I will let you leave with a handful of gold, but you must promise to never speak of what you saw here or where you got the gold."

"And if I don't get any correct?" Peter questioned suspiciously.

"Well… then… I will kill you."

Peter stood for a moment and thought about the dragon's offer. Up until that point, he'd only heard stories of the cunning and deceitfulness of dragons. He knew his fate was in the dragon's hands and that his only option was to play its game, so he agreed.

"Okay, Dragon. I will play your game, but you have to promise to let me leave if I get one of your questions correct."

"I will let you leave if you get one correct,' the dragon shot back arrogantly. "If you somehow best me, I will honor my word and let you leave. You will have to answer all my questions though."

"Okay, dragon. I'll play your game. Let's begin. What are your three questions?"

CHAPTER 26:

THE PRINCE & PETER PT. 2

Oliver Burke

When Oliver peered over, he saw Bastian's tears had cleared and the child was staring intently at his storytelling. He could tell, like his own, that Bastian's attention was momentarily diverted away from the horrific last scene they both shared with Lenny during his cardiac arrest. His plan was working.

I can't send this kid to the foster care system. I can't. Amerie never experienced it and she doesn't understand. I'm not sure what this will mean for us, but I need to be here for Bas.

Before he continued, Oliver peered over and noticed the hospital room door was slightly ajar. Unlike him, Bastian did not notice it and when he looked over, his look softened as he connected eyes with Amerie and saw her smiling back. She didn't enter the room, just stood outside to show her support for what Oliver, Bastian, and Lenny, were going through.

She came. Wow. She came, he thought to himself. Her eyes were tearful, and he watched as she mouthed, '*I love you,*' silently before turning away back to her seat in the hallway. He smiled at the thought of her support and continued with the story.

"If you answer one of three questions correctly, you win. If you don't, you lose and will be my prisoner. Okay?

"Okay, Dragon. I'll play your game."

"Okay, boy," the dragon began. "Your first question is what is the name of this cave?"

Peter could not recall seeing the cave on any maps and when he ran through the forest, he did not remember which direction he took. He was unsure where he was exactly and used a few moments to deliberate on the answer. When he saw the dragon growing impatient, he forced an answer.

"This is the Brockland cave," he said confidently.

"Wrong!" The dragon responded in excitement. "This cave is unnamed so you're wrong, boy! Second question. What is the difference between sunrise and sunset?"

Peter didn't have many friends his age in town and often found himself speaking to the tradesmen. He recalled a conversation he had with the local baker about his opening and closing hours, and confidently answered the dragon with credence.

"Sunrise is the time in the morning where the sun appears, and sunset is when the sun disappears in the evening."

The dragon stood silent and vexed. He threw Peter a murderous stare and exhaled a cloud of smoke.

"Dragon? Is that correct?"

"Yes," the dragon admitted shortly. "That's correct."

Peter jumped for joy. He was thrilled he'd answered a question correctly and at the thought that he'd won the dragon's game. The thought that he'd bested the dragon made him joyful.

"I did as you instructed and got one correct. Now let me pass with my gold. You'll never hear from me again, dragon. You can trust me."

"You still have one more question, boy. I said there would be three and you still have one remaining."

"Why would I need to answer the third if I've already answered one correctly? That doesn't make any sense."

"Those are the rules, boy. You have one last question," the dragon sneered back before continuing to his third and final question. "What is the name of the largest and wealthiest village?"

Peter was equally excited and confused at the question. Everyone knew Brockland was the largest and wealthiest village around so he was puzzled at why the dragon would make the final question so easy for him, especially since he'd answered a previous question with Brockland in his answer. He was smart and could tell the dragon was cunning but assumed he'd already earned his freedom and disregarded any further thoughts of trickery. He answered the dragon.

"The largest and wealthiest village in the area is Brockland? Brockland is my answer," Peter said confidently.

"That is correct, boy!" The dragon responded with a contrived smile.

"Okay, enough games, dragon. I've answered two of your questions correctly. It's time for me to go."

"You're not going anywhere, boy. I said you only needed one of three questions correct…but you answered two correctly…which means you lose."

"Dragon, you promised me gold and freedom. Why are you going against your word?"

"I promised no such thing, boy. You've lost and are now my prisoner. The only thing I'll promise you is if you try to leave, I will rain fire on your village and all the silly people who live there. This is my game and I've created the rules." The dragon then paused, momentarily deliberating in his head then continued. "I'll give you another chance to buy your freedom, but you'll have to play a new game. In this game, you will get 10 questions a day and I will give you one coin for all questions you get correct. For any questions you get wrong, I will take a gold coin back. Your freedom will cost you 100 coins and I will start you off with a bag of 51 coins. If your bag becomes empty, you will be stuck here forever – no more games."

"How do I know you aren't deceiving me again, dragon?"

"You question me, boy! Do you not forget I'm letting you start with an advantage of 51 coins? That's your only reassurance. Once you have 100 coins, you can put them into the lock, and it will unlock the door to your freedom. No more games."

Peter was trembling in fear. The dragon's true self had finally revealed itself and he'd realized his mistake. He knew he should've never come to the cave and deliberated. Given the dragon's sly tongue, Peter knew he was out of options and agreed to play the game. His fate was set, and he was ready.

The dragon led Peter down one of the long, dark hallways to his space. The space was large, like the rest of the cave, and was also poorly lit. It had a door that locked from the outside and when the dragon shoved Peter through it, he dropped the half-filled bag of gold at Peter's feet and locked the door behind him. When the dragon was gone, Peter went to one corner of the room and began to cry.

"Why did the dragon lie to him?" Bastian questioned.

"Well, he didn't lie to him technically. He tricked him with half-truths."

"What's that?"

"It's a deceptive statement that includes a small bit of the truth to entice you but it's mostly false. People usually use it when they want to trick you."

"Why did the dragon do that?"

"Because the dragon was no good. It was used to winning and did not accept the fact that a boy had beat it in its own game. The dragon was proud and couldn't see past its ego. Its selfishness was like venom and when it spoke, the boy could hardly tell the difference between the truths and the lies. It all sounded the same, but the boy knew he was stuck. Participation was his only chance of survival."

Oliver paused then cleared his throat. He felt himself raising his voice as he spoke about the vile creature and stopped to exhale. "Sadly, there are people like this in real life also. I hope you never have to run into someone like the dragon, Bas. They promise you gold and freedom, but they only trick you."

"What happened after Peter was locked in the room?"

Well…while he cried on the floor of the dark space, he thought heard a voice come from the opposite corner. The voice called to him so faintly that Peter almost missed it but as he sat at attention, he knew it was a boy's voice he was hearing. It was still very dark in the room and Peter could barely see his own feet in front of him, so he crawled towards the feeble voice until it was right in front of him.

"Who are you?" Peter questioned.

The voice was gravelly and harsh. "Do you have any water? I need water."

Peter still had his knapsack from his journey and pulled out one of the pouched filled with water. Gripping it, he extended his arm until the pack was pulled from his grip by the mysterious stranger. He could hear the boy slurping the water.

"'Hey! Leave some for me too,' Peter shot back."

"Sorry," the voice responded clearing his throat. 'Thank you. 'What's your name?"

"My name is Peter. Who are you?"

"Prince Nelson is my name."

"Prince Nelson?" Peter shot back in confusion. "We all thought you were dead?"

"Almost…" the prince countered. "I probably would have died of dehydration if you hadn't given me that water. Thank you, Peter. How long have I been here?"

"You've been missing for almost a year. Everyone was looking for you. When we couldn't find you, we all assumed you died. Is this where you've been?"

"Yes, Peter. I've been the dragon's prisoner since the day I disappeared. Why are you here?"

"I ran away and came to this cave. When I entered, the dragon saw me and made me play its game. It tricked me and I lost. Now I'm a prisoner."

"That's how the dragon got me also," the prince admitted. "With promises of gold and freedom, right? The dragon doesn't want you to be free. It wants you to play its game and keep it entertained. You'll never win. Did the dragon also tell you that your freedom will cost you 100 coins?"

"Yes, it did."

"It told me that also. I've won some days but lost most. It manipulated the questions to ensure I never won and on the days I got all 10 questions correct, the dragon starved me and deprived me of water. The last time it came here, I was so weak I couldn't even play the game. The dragon must have thought I died and turned its attention to you. How many coins do you have Peter?"

"The dragon started me off with 51 coins?"

"51?"

Peter could hear the confusion in the prince's tone. "Yes – 51. The dragon tried to convince me that it was doing me a favor but deep down, I know it's another game I'm supposed to lose."

"Okay, Peter – Last I checked, I had about 41 coins, which means you now have 92. If you can win just one day of the dragon's trickery, you can buy your freedom."

"'My freedom?' Peter questioned. 'What about you?'"

"Truth be told, I'm not planning on being here much longer," the prince admitted. "If you hadn't shown up, I probably would be dead and now I'm too weak to run. You need to take my coins and save yourself. I won't make it."

"I can't leave you, Prince Nelson. I won't leave you…"

At that same moment, the Prince and Peter could hear the dragon unlocking their cell. The prince whispered something in Peter's ear and then shoved him backward. "Go!"

Peter looked up just as the dragon unlocked the door and the prince faded back into the darkness.

"Are you ready to play?" the dragon jeered as it looked over.

"Yes — I'm ready, dragon. No more games. Tell me your ten questions and no more tricks."

"You don't give orders here," the dragon roared in response.

"Okay, okay. I mean you no offense. I'm tired and just want to go home. Please let's begin. What is your first question?"

CHAPTER 27:

THE PRINCE & PETER PT. 3

Oliver Burke

"What happened to the Prince?" Bastian questioned. "Did Peter just leave him while he answered the dragon's questions?

"Oh no! The prince did something very brave and noble for Peter that day. He sacrificed his coins in hopes of Peter winning his freedom. He knew he didn't have the strength to continue and left Peter with the one advantage he knew the dragon couldn't take from either of them. We all have people in our lives like the prince. People who'll sacrifice everything so we can make it. So we can break from a broken cycle of pain and poverty." Oliver continued.

"Fortunately, Peter already had intellect, but he welcomed any additional help he could get. The dragon was cunning, so Peter needed to be cunning too. Before the door opened, the prince also left him with one message, which he'd whispered in Peter's ear moments before the dragon entered the room."

"What was the message?" Bastian questioned anxiously. "What did he tell him?"

"That's the good part! The next part of the story will reveal what happened," Oliver replied. When he peered over, he saw Bastian yawn and knew he wasn't far from sleep. His sitting position was now more of a slouch, and he began rubbing his eyes with balled fists.

When the dragon entered, it looked over in the corner and saw the prince's still-body and turned his attention back to Peter.

"Okay, boy. We'll now begin the game. Your first question... What is the name of a baby goat?"

"A Buck or a Billy," Peter quickly responded. "Next question."

"That is correct. Question number two...how many days are in a year?"

"There are three hundred sixty-five days in a year."

"Also correct," the Dragon scoffed.

"Question number three...what is a leap year?"

"A leap year is a year where there is an extra day added to the shortest month – which means February would have 29 days instead of the normal 28 days."

"Correct again..."

At this point, Peter had answered the dragon's first three questions correctly and he could tell the dragon was growing angry. The dragon didn't know this but he only needed a total of 8 coins to reach his goal of 100 and realized he needed to adjust his approach to beat the dragon at his game. He had to use the dragon's own rules of trickery to beat it before it could change the rules.

"Question number four...how many feet are there in a mile?"

Peter knew the correct answer was 5,280 feet but also knew he needed to mislead the dragon into thinking he didn't know the correct answer—to save the dragon's pride and ego. For the sake of his freedom, he couldn't make the dragon think he was winning because the dragon was very proud and would increase the difficulty of the questions as his control of the situation decreased. Peter saw it as a critical factor between his freedom or continued imprisonment. 'There are 5,000 feet in a mile..."

"Wrong!" The dragon shot back in satisfaction. "That is wrong! There are 5,280 feet in a mile."

The dragon believed he'd regained control of the situation and continued. "Questions number five, six, and seven...How many seasons are there? What are they and what is my favorite season?"

Peter could tell the dragon was attempting to deceive him with the last question. He knew what the seasons were and took a chance on the dragon's trick question. "There are four seasons, dragon. They are fall, winter, spring, and summer. I don't know how I'm supposed to know your favorite season, but I will say the summer."

Peter could see the contempt growing on the dragon's face as he answered the three questions correctly. "Is that correct?"

"Yes, boy. That's correct," he scowled back. "Question eight... what is a fish that can breathe on land?"

Peter sat bewildered.

"An octopus?"

"Wrong!" The gratification had returned to the dragon's face as it looked down on Peter. The imprisoned teen had answered only six of his eight questions correctly and two incorrect which meant he had only won four coins. The dragon assumed there was no way he could win and smiled in satisfaction. What the dragon didn't know was how close Peter really was to his freedom— thanks to the prince.

"You've only won four coins and your final two questions... How many legs does a spider have? What is a doe?"

Peter stood for a moment... "Spiders have eight legs, and a doe is a female deer."

"That is correct, boy," the dragon derided contentedly. "You've only answered eight of the ten questions correctly and two incorrectly which means you lose for today and you're still my prisoner! Tomorrow, the questions will be tougher."

Just before the dragon swiftly departed the room, Peter yelled.

"Wait, dragon. Why not make today's questions tougher? Those you gave were easy and surely you have something harder?"

It stood silent in apprehension. The dragon believed it had outsmarted Peter and grew livid at his ridicule. It refused to accept the fact that Peter had outsmarted and scoffed at his challenge.

"I will give you another question for today, boy. This will be double the amount. If you answer it correctly, you get two coins. If you answer it incorrectly, you lose two coins. Do we have a deal?"

"Deal!" Peter shot back confidently.

"If you suffer from pyrophobia, what are you afraid of?"

Peter stared into the dragon's eyes as he considered the question. In its deep, dark pupils, Peter saw nothing but darkness, and through the darkness, there was a burning desire. He could sense something deeper to the question and believed the dragon held contentment in the answer."

"Someone who suffers from pyrophobia is afraid of fire."

The dragon shot fire into the air in frustration as it dropped eight coins onto the ground and stormed out of the room. It said nothing and locked the door behind it as it disappeared. Peter crawled back over to the corner where he'd left the prince and called out for him. There was a silence, so Peter continued to crawl until he ran into the prince's still body. He shook the body but there was no response. He continued to shake the body until the prince finally opened his eyes and looked back at Peter.

"Did we win?" he said weakly.

"Yes, we won! We're getting out of here. We're going home."

Peter mounted the prince's body on his feeble shoulders, displaying a strength he'd never shown before, and motioned towards the locked door. He used all 100 of their coins to unlock it and passed through. The cave was dim, so he walked slowly and after ambling in the darkness for minutes, he finally found the entrance and they fled through it. Before disappearing back into the forest to get back to Brockland, Peter knew he needed to do something to avoid others from falling victim to the dragon's tactics. He decided to trap the dragon in its lair so he could live *the rest of his days with all the gold he desired. Sort of like a punishment for the dragon's greed.*

Peter saw a large boulder beside the cave entrance and attempted to move it to cover the entrance. Despite his enormous will, the boulder was too heavy for him alone and he struggled and struggled. He knew he need to do something and continued to exert all his strength. The prince saw this and slowly rose to his feet, then made his way behind Peter. He too mustered up all the remaining strength he had left and together, they were able to move the boulder—finally trapping the dragon.

"We did it!" Peter replied in excitement. "The dragon's trapped and we can finally go home."

There was a silence as Peter looked behind him. On the ground, the prince laid stiff and still. Peter continued to call out his name but the prince—

At that moment, Oliver turned his attention to Bastian, who was now deeply asleep and smiled at the child's innocence. He wasn't sure when Bastian had fallen asleep but knew he would have to retell at least a portion of the story—and grinned cheerfully. As he watched, Oliver silently recited to himself.

"The world didn't accept Peter, so he ran…

The prince was trapped, so he made a sacrifice…

The fire-breathing dragon tricked them both because of its greed. Because of his greed…

This is my story. I think I know what I need to do. I know what you need me to do…"

At the same moment, Oliver finished his last thought, Amerie slowly and quietly entered the room. As she approached, Oliver noticed her eyes were puffy as she traded glances between him and Bastian.

Wow. She must've been in the hallway all night. She must've been listening to the story.

Without saying a word, Amerie went straight up to Oliver and wrapped her arms around him tightly. She kissed him and whispered in his ear, "I'm so sorry."

Oliver felt the wetness of her cheeks and held back his tears. A ball had formed in his throat as he attempted to find words but struggled. He continued to embrace her until he was finally able to clear his throat and find his voice. He whispered.

"I can't believe you're here. You really didn't have to but I'm so happy to see you."

"I wanted to come," she replied as she held her palm against his face. "There's nowhere else I'd rather be right now than here with the two of you."

"This is Bastian. Lenny's grandson."

"He's so precious. You two look good together. I can tell he's comfortable with you. How's Lenny doing?"

Oliver peered down at Bastian and saw he was still asleep, so he continued.

"He's already been through so much. Lenny had a pretty bad cardiac attack earlier today and they sent him to another room. Now, they're observing him closely to try to get him back, but I don't know what's going to happen to him," Oliver leaned in and whispered. "I don't know what's going to happen but... I'm all Bastian has right now."

Amerie looked over at Bastian, then back to Oliver with a meaningful gaze.

"No, babe...He has both of us. We're in this together."

Oliver froze and looked at her with wide-eyes. He felt a heavy feeling in his stomach and stared at her without blinking. With his wide eyes, he saw a smile form on her face and gave her one back.

"Wait…Are you serious?"

"Yes, I am. Before you left, you said Lenny wasn't doing too well and I thought more about what you shared about his story."

Oliver continued to stare with hopeful eyes which were now on the verge of tears.

"Both of you made it on the backs of good women. Now I'm here for you too."

"Thank you, thank you, thank you! I think we can do it."

"No, I know we can. We've always figured it out together."

Oliver smiled as he peered over at the clock on the wall then down at Bastian. "It's already so late and I need to stay here with Bas until we get an update on Lenny. You should head home and get some rest before work in the morning."

"You sure? I can stay if you need me to."

"No, that's okay. I'm not sure how much longer this will be. I'll keep you updated on everything. I love you."

"Okay, my love. I love you too. I'll head home. But make sure your phone's charged," she joked as they traded kisses.

Right before she departed, Amerie looked at Oliver and asked. "I have one question though. About the story. What did the prince whisper to Peter?"

Oliver held jubilation in his eyes as he looked into hers. "He said, I will not allow you to also die at the hands of this monster. This is the last thing I want to leave you with. Peace of mind to know you're free and be safe."

Amerie erupted and Oliver's eyes flooded at the sign of her tears. He had rapid breaths which made him unable to continue. He covered his eyes with one hand and attempted to speak but could only produce sounds that resembled words. Amerie leaned in to hold him tightly and they cried on each other's shoulders. "It's okay, honey. It's okay," she offered.

Oliver continued to hold her until they finally slowed their tears and he found his voice. "That's what Ma told me."

She looked at Oliver and used her sleeves to wipe his tears before wiping her own. She kissed his lips and stood to her feet.

"I'll see you and Bastian at home. I love you so much."

After she departed, Oliver saw Bastian was still deep asleep and brought him close. He kissed the crown of his head and just held him. He wasn't sure what was going on with Lenny but as far as he knew it, he had Bastian covered. He pulled the Black Panther blanket over them both, also closed his eyes, and drifted into sleep.

CHAPTER 28:

WHO WILL REMEMBER ME WHEN I'M GONE?

Oliver Burke

By the next morning, Oliver was awoken by the nurses rolling Lenny's frail body back into the hospital room. It had been roughly sixteen hours since he'd seen him last but Lenny looked much weaker than he remembered. It was obvious that he was hours, maybe even minutes, from death and his fear assailed him. When he looked down, he saw Bastian was still sound asleep, so he slid from underneath his still body over to Lenny's bedside.

Lenny was still sleeping when the nurses left the room, but Oliver grabbed his cold hand and silently said a prayer for his friend. He bowed his head, closed his eyes, and began.

Seconds into the prayer, Lenny finally opened his eyes and interrupted. "Hey man," he said weakly.

"You're up. How do you feel?"

"Like I'm dying. Thanks for being here. Where's Bas?"

"He's still sleeping on the couch," Oliver began to get choked up. "Man, it's so hard to see you like this. I can't imagine what you're going through."

"I feel like my heart's been ripped out of my chest and I died and came back to life. Truth be told, we could sit here and talk about how I'm doing but I don't know how much longer I have. There's one last thing I need to do before the end." He coughed to clear his throat. Lenny looked over at Bastian and his eyebrows formed a grimace. "Do you know what you're going to do?"

"I don't know if I'm ready to lose you. I just got you back and now you're going to leave us again. Lenny, I don't wanna lose you."

"Oliver… our stories were written long before we knew they were. Everything that's happened. Everything we've been through. Was for this very moment. Sadly, this is where my story ends and hopefully, yours gets better. Before I go, I *need* to know my grandson is cared for. Are you and Amerie going to take Bas?"

"…Yes Lenny. We are. We talked about it and prayed about it. I won't lie to you; I wasn't sure if this was the right decision for us or if this was even for me. There's been a lot that's happened over my life that made me question if I could have done more… Now I have the chance to do more—for you—and I want to do it. He'll have a home with us."

"Really?"

"Yes. This is the least we can do."

There was an immense exhale from Lenny followed by an ear-to-ear smile.

"Thank you, thank you, thank you… I can't thank you enough. I haven't told Bas what's happening yet, but I've talked a lot about you. We never had much, just each other so there isn't much to pass over. All he'll need is your love." Lenny paused to clear his throat. "I think we should talk to him together. I think that's best. This won't be easy for any of us but it's something we'll need to do. Would now work for you?"

"Oh wow. So soon? I didn't prepare anything," Oliver remarked. "Should I go grab something from the gift shop? Would another time work better?"

"Leap of faith, right? We may not have a better time than right now. If our history has shown us anything, we need to do the things we want and say the things we need to today because we don't know about tomorrow."

"That's true. Let's do it now... together."

Oliver went to turn around to wake up Bastian but froze. "Wait..." He searched Lenny's starry eyes for any hope he could find that this would not be his final ending. When his friend looked back, Oliver only saw acceptance beaming in his glare and asked, "How do you want him to remember you?"

"I want him to remember me as someone who gave it my all. Every day I did what I could. I know it was not enough but I tried."

"I'll ensure he never forgets that. Neither of us will."

Oliver went to wake Bastian up, who wiped the sleep from his eyes and rushed over to Lenny's side when he saw he was awake.

"Hey, my big boy. I missed you so much."

"Grandpa. Are you going to die?"

Both Oliver and Lenny stood silent.

"Hey, lil man. We need to talk to you about something important."

Oliver watched as Lenny cupped his young face in his frail hands.

"Look, Bas – you are the best thing that's ever happened to me. You've been my road dog since you were in diapers and now, you're a growing boy. My big boy. I'm so proud of you. For seven years, you've been

245

my sunshine and my shadow." Lenny caught himself getting choked up and paused. He squeezed the inner corners of his eyes with his thumb and forefinger and held this for seconds as he cleared his throat.

"Remember when you were five and lost your first tooth? Remember what I told you?"

"Yes. You said my weak tooth had to go so a stronger tooth can grow there."

"Exactly, and it's already grown so much. My beautiful boy. Look at you. Just like your mother."

Lenny paused again and traded glances over to Oliver. He was still fighting back tears and his voice continued to break. He turned back to Bastian and stared before continuing.

"Well, Bas, I need to go away soon. Just like your tooth. It's almost my time to go so someone stronger can come in and you can be *their* road dog."

"What do you mean? Where are you going? Are you coming back?"

Lenny's eyes now filled with tears as he fought to keep them back. He failed and watched as Bastian also began tearing up.

"No...I don't think I'll be able to come back this time. That's why my *best* friend in the whole world is here. He's going to take my place and you'll now be his best friend in the world. His road-dog..."

"But... can I go with you, grandpa? Please? I wanna go with you," Bastian replied, his voice cracking after each word.

The tears Lenny held back were now flowing as he choked on his words. A tightening of his throat and a short intake of his breaths suddenly appeared as he covered his eyes with his weak hands.

"No, Bas. I'm sorry. Where I'm going, you and Oliver can't come. I need you to be strong. My life was hard and..." Lenny paused and kept his eyes covered to hide his deep grief and sorrow. "...I had to be strong, but you made it all worth it. Every day was worth it with you. All the best moments of my life were with you."

It was at that very moment that Lenny grabbed Bastian, who was also now crying uncontrollably, and used his frail hands to wipe his tears. He brought him close and held him tight. He held him tighter than he'd ever held him before in hopes of leaving him with this one fleeting memory. A memory of a love that filled their stomachs every night when money couldn't. He whispered something in Bastian's ear and Oliver watched as Bastian lowered his head, closed his eyes, and the two of them silently recited in unison.

Lenny then retracted his body and looked into Bastian's eyes. "Oliver will care for you and even though you won't see me, I'll always be with you both. I love you so much."

Oliver then leaned in to embrace the two of them and they all sobbed loudly. Nothing else mattered at that moment. No words were said, and Oliver could tell Bastian was attempting to make sense of it all. The child stood silent with a perplexed look on his face.

Although he was still figuring things out, Oliver could sense Bastian knew more about Lenny's sickness than he let on but the shock of losing anyone had finally sprung upon him. He knew he needed to be present for the child and gripped him tighter to show his support. They held their embrace and let their tears run until Lenny finally retracted his body and looked at them both—eyes still puffy and wet.

"I think it's time for me to go to sleep now. I love you both so much and will never… ever… forget you or leave you. I'll always be there in the moments you need me…that I promise.

"Bas, be strong and be a good boy for Oliver. He'll watch over you like I did, and care for you. He'll love you this much," Lenny said stretching his arms out for a big hug. "I love you so much, my big boy. You are everything and in the moments you feel sad or lonely, please put your hands together like I showed you and say your prayers. I'll be listening every time." He then turned his attention to Oliver.

"Please don't forget me. Until we can all be together again, please remember me. Please. I love you, man. I'll see you on the other side."

"We love you too, Lenny," Oliver remarked wiping his face. "Thank *you* for finding me. You changed things for me also and I wish we had more time. I'm so mad that it took us thirty years to see each other again and wish I could change things but I'm glad for every second we did have together. This isn't goodbye. Definitely feels more like a see you later. I find it hard to believe we were brought back together after *all* this time just to have it end like this. No way. I'll def see you later… when we *both* make it home."

"Home sounds good," Lenny stated as he began to drift.

Oliver then kissed Lenny's forehead and looked at Bastian, who wore his enormous sorrow. The child still had tears flowing from his eyes and simply placed his small hand in Oliver's. Lenny saw this and smiled as he drifted into his final sleep.

*****

As they exited the room, Oliver connected eyes with the doctor whom he'd spoken with previously and got choked up. The doctor and nurses wore sympathy on their faces and stood silent as he approached with Bastian trailing closely behind him.

"He's gone," Oliver remarked with sadness. "Thank you for giving us one last moment together."

"I'm very sorry about your brother. I can't imagine what the two of you are going through."

Bastian's eyes were still wet and puffy, so Oliver squeezed his hand and watched as the hospital staff entered the room to check on his now-deceased friend. He mustered all the strength he could find and used his free hand to wipe Bastian's eyes.

For seven years, Lenny had been his sole provider and now entrusted Oliver with the well-being of his grandson. He did not take this responsibility lightly and wanted him to know he would always be there for him.

"Don't worry, Bas."

When he looked down at him, he thought back to the last sight of his best friend before his passing. The smile which he knew hid a pain he could never fully understand and the watery eyes which held tears filled with acceptance and gratitude.

We've been trading things our whole life, man, he thought to himself as he continued to stare at Bastian. *Now you can rest easy knowing you're free and Bas has a home. Rest easy, my friend.*

He smiled.

"Bas – I loved your grandfather and will miss him so much. The story I shared with you tells pieces of our past that made us who we are. As time goes on, I plan to tell you everything because I think you'll need to hear it. My mother used to say honesty is our credit to heaven. She would tell me this and reminded me to always say my prayers because someone was always watching. I saw you and Lenny say a prayer. It was beautiful."

Oliver used his sleeve to wipe the tears still falling from Bastian's eyes and continued.

"I can never replace him in your life but hope to bring you the same joy he brought. If you're okay with it, I would love to pray with you next time. We can even say a prayer for grandpa."

"It wasn't a prayer we said," Bastian traded. "Grandpa told me to remember a poem he used to tell me before bed."

And then, from the most joyful corners of his memory, rises the poem that carried him to sleep every night. Two lines of poetry and Lenny's final farewell to him:

Although the scars were meant to show stories of defeat, ...the wounds healed,
The deepest damages done are often the ones they don't see,
But the ones that they do see are meant to show how they couldn't break us.
We overcame.

The End

Topics and Questions for Discussions:

1. What does *'Scars Serve As Reminders'* mean to you?"

2. A Rumi quote, *"The wound is the place where the Light enters you,"* was referenced in the beginning of the book. How did we see this throughout the novel?

3. Over the course of the three novels, we see several scenes more than once such as the graveyard scene, when Lenny and Oliver meet, and the flashbacks with Eugene Garry, Peter Castile, and Tremaine Morgan. What were those intended to highlight in each novel?

4. The book cover of *'Scars Serves As Reminders'* gives a brief visual into the books ending. Why give away the books ending in this way?

5. When Lenny finishes the recount of his life, he makes a comment about "running his whole life." In what ways was Lenny running?

6. Oliver and Lenny hadn't known each other that long before Lenny went missing. How did Lenny's disappearance affect Oliver so deeply?

7. Describe the changes seen in Oliver between ANGELS and SCARS.

8. The Cycle of Grief is described in five stages. **Denial, Anger, Bargaining, Depression,** and **Acceptance**. At what points of the novel did we find Lenny in each stage?

9. Consider Lenny's relationship with Rahzmel. Why did he fight so hard for his cousins approval despite knowing who he was and what he was involved in?

10. Although Lenny wasn't sure Oliver would take Bastian, he still continued to smoke. What was the symbolism in that?

11. The story *The Prince & Peter* held several similarities to Lenny & Oliver's stories. Why did Oliver choose to tell Bastian this story when Lenny chose to avoid it?

12. This novel was broken up into three parts. What were the general themes of each of these segments of the novel?

AFTERWORD

For over eight years, the story of Oliver Burke has maintained residency in my mind. Through my encounters, shared laughs, moments of distress, tears, insomnia and heartbreak… the story came to life. Writing this trilogy was the greatest journey of my life because it allowed me to research the complexities of human beings. The one question that I found myself asking at each turn was why? Why do we do what we do?

In our lives, there are people who will serve a greater purpose towards the men and women we choose to become. People who lose their way, like Walter Benine, and need to be reminded why they matter. People like Rahzmel Davis who thrive off the weaknesses of others and use it against them. People like Lenny McNair, who root and pray for us even in the moments we may not see or hear them. But most importantly, there are people like Mabel-Ara Burke, who give us a love without any reservations or requisites, and help us believe in the impossible. It highlights the people we became and the people we were saved from… even when we may not have realized it.

Although the character of Oliver Burke is fictional, he represents more than just a man or a figure. Oliver Burke represents the inherent realities of purpose, care, love and loss that we all encounter in our lives. He's defined by perseverance and the concept of paying it forward. He chose to change the lives of others because others changed his life. His why was because he could never forget the people and moments that changed his life.

As you read: **The Purposeful Oliver Burke**, **The Angels Are Flying So Low**, and **Scars Serve as Reminders**, consider your life, and the moments you chose to play the role of Mabel-Ara, Lenny or Oliver Burke for someone else. Think about the battle's they're fighting without any clear indication of their pain, and do the most important step of them all - act. You'll sleep better at night and the future's counting on you.

Will Appiah
May, 2022

Made in the USA
Middletown, DE
21 August 2022